I0549233

Mrs. Cantrel Whirled Around at Jennifer's Gasp.

Jennifer grabbed Marysue's arm and sprinted frantically for the trees, not saying anything. She had no idea how long it took, could only hear her own footsteps, and imagined the teacher, Mrs. Gantrel, closing the gap.

Then Jennifer saw the clearing at last, and she stopped, held her stomach and gulped for air.

She heard nothing.

The woods were silent.

"What did you see?" Marysue asked then, and when Jennifer told her, the blood drained from her face. "You're kidding, right?"

"No. I wish I was."

"A trick of the light. It had to be."

Jennifer nodded at the possibility.

It had to be. Otherwise, Mrs. Gantrel's hand was covered with fur.

iBooks in the **PRIVATE SCHOOL**™ Series

Most iBooks are available at special quantity discounts for bulk purchases for sales promotions, premiums or fundraising. Special books or book excerpts can also be created to fit specific needs.
For details, email the publisher
@bricktower@aol.com

PRIVATE SCHOOL #1 Nightmare Session

Steven Charles

A BYRON PREISS VISUAL PUBLICATIONS, INC. BOOK

iBooks for Young Readers
Habent Sua Fata Libelli

iBooks
Manhanset House
Dering Harbor, New York 11965

bricktower@aol.com • www.ibooksinc.com

All rights reserved under the International and Pan-American
Copyright Conventions. Printed in the United States by J. Boylston &
Company, Publishers, New York. No part of this publication may be
reproduced, stored in a retrieval system, or transmitted in any form or by
any means, electronic, or otherwise, without the prior written permission
of the copyright holder. The iBooks colophon is a trademark of
J. Boylston & Company, Publishers.

Copyright © 1986 by Byron Preiss Visual Publications
Cover artwork copyright © 1986 by Gary Lang c/o Jerry Leff Associates
PRIVATE SCHOOL is a trademark of Byron Preiss Visual Publications

Library of Congress Cataloging-in-Publication Data
Charles, Steven. Nightmare Sessions.
        (Private School) "A Byron Preiss book."
p. cm.
        [1. Young Adult Fiction—Horror. 2. Young Adult Fiction—Science
Fiction—Alien Contact. 3. Young Adult Fiction—Werewolfs and
Shifters.] I. Lang, Gary, ill. II. Title. III.
        Series: Charles, Steven. Private School.

ISBN 978-1-59687-730-6
November 2018

SPECIAL THANKS TO RON BUEHL,
PAT MACDONALD, MARJORIE HANLON,
AND DAVID M. HARRIS.
EDITOR—RUTH ASHBY

NIGHTMARE
SESSION

Table of Contents

Table of Contents

Chapter One

JENNIFER WAS WORRIED.

Not only was she asking for trouble by being off campus, but the weather was about to complicate her problems. The late-August sky was swiftly filling with massive thunderheads, and it was going to rain before she made it back to the dorm, and the one thing she couldn't afford now was a summer cold.

"Hey, Field, c'mon!" a voice hissed, and she started, blinked, and rushed to catch up with the others.

There were four of them, hurrying along the north end of a ten-foot-high brick wall that enclosed Thaler Academy on three sides. Despite the narrow path worn through the underbrush, the way was rough—shrubs and close-set trees had them batting aside branches as if they were in a jungle, and twice Jennifer stumbled over a root hidden in the ivy that covered the ground as well as the brick.

Someone up ahead muttered a curse, someone else laughed, and finally Monica Holt whispered, "Eureka!"

Jennifer didn't bother to conceal a sigh of relief, but winced when she heard the rusted hinges of an iron gate shriek as they opened. No one knew why the gate was there, so far from the main entrance, but it had been discovered years before by students looking for an unobservable way into town. Going into Staines was not against the rules during the regular school year, but it was actively discouraged while summer classes were in session, a time when students were supposed to be getting a jump on the coming year or making up poor grades.

Quickly the girls slipped through the opening, emerging into a stand of massive evergreens, whose wide swaying boughs kept the air beneath in twilight and even darker now as the clouds converged, turning the summer afternoon to threatening midnight.

The hinges shrieked again as the gate was pushed shut.

The others moved on, whispering and giggling, but Jennifer held back a moment, until her eyes adjusted. It was so dark that she could barely see through the trees to her dormitory, two stories of red brick and white trim in the colonial style, less than a hundred yards from the edge of the trees.

Thunder rumbled.

The air grew damp and unpleasantly cool.

Then a gust of wind kicked a spinning cloud of dust into the air, and she turned away from it just as someone gave an all-clear whistle. The others pounded across the grass, but as she dodged a low-hanging branch, she tripped over an unseen rock and sprawled on the ground, gasping when the air was knocked from her lungs. She rolled onto her back, unable to cry out, hugging herself and gulping until at last she was able to take a clear breath.

Dumb, Field, she told herself when she finally pushed herself to her feet. Truly dumb.

She rubbed a hand across the flat of her chest to ease the dull ache and inhaled slowly, deeply, abruptly aware of how silent the late afternoon had grown. The wind had paused, the thunder had stopped, and there was nothing now but the sound of her breathing—and something moving behind her.

She didn't want to turn around.

She knew, she just knew that with her luck, it would be Peter Dramon, the dean of students, ready to catch her and throw her out of school.

A twig snapped.

She started forward, thinking she could pretend she was only out for a walk, that there was no way the dean could prove she had broken the rules.

Thunder again, louder.

Whoever was there was moving with her, on her right and only a few yards away.

A strange noise, like the scuffing of a shoe in dead pine needles or the snuffling of a wild beast.

She ducked under a branch, the needles teasing her hair, and as she neared the lawn she wondered why the man didn't call out her name, didn't stop her, didn't accuse her.

Maybe, she thought then, it wasn't the dean at all.

And she grinned to herself.

Of course not. It was Monica Holt. She hadn't run to the dorm at all but had circled around and ducked back into the trees, hoping to sneak up behind her and give her a scare.

The grin widened.

A deep-throated animal growling reached her. It was hokey, but just Monica's style.

And just as she turned to confront her, lightning flared and the storm broke.

On the heels of deafening thunder that echoed endlessly through the hills, the wind bellowed out of the black sky, turning the branches to whips, kicking dust and grit from the ground and slapping it against her face. She was nearly knocked off her feet and started running as soon as her balance returned.

Monica could get soaked for all she cared now; all she wanted to do was get to the safety of the dorm.

Lightning crackled.

The thunder so loud she clamped her hands to her ears.

The wind so strong that as she reached the edge of the trees it turned her around.

The rain thrumming against the ground, churning the dust into mud. And she heard it, muffled by all the sounds of the storm but still unmistakably a howling.

And she saw it in the next flash of blue white.

Something.

Standing under a pine tree, half hidden by the branches and the wind's rushing shadows, caught in the lightning's glare, and staring at her.

The light faded so quickly she couldn't make out the thing's features, and when another bolt ripped through the clouds it was gone, nothing but darkness left, nothing left but the wind.

Jennifer stared at the spot where she had seen it, squinting against the wind, her hair lashing across her face.

Then, suddenly, she turned and ran.

Not from the storm, or the rain, but from the thing she had seen.

It wasn't Monica, and it wasn't the dean.

Whatever it was, she knew it wasn't human.

By the time she reached the second floor, Jennifer was ready to laugh at herself. Though she freely admitted to having a pretty fair imagination, seeing monsters creeping around on a private school campus in Connecticut was stretching things a bit far, even for her.

Her room was in the comer at the back, and she hurried down the gold-and-green painted hall without meeting anyone, pushed open the door, and stumbled in breathlessly. Then she closed the door behind her and sagged wearily against it, shaking her head at her foolishness.

Monsters, she thought.

"Monsters," she said aloud and rolled her eyes at the sound of it.

Though it had seemed real, she knew it had to have been only a trick of the light—a tree trunk or a bush the lightning had turned into a creature. The flash had come and gone so quickly there had been no time to focus properly, and under the circumstances she probably would have thought a fallen branch was a giant snake.

Nerves, that's what it was.

It couldn't have been anything else.

Nerves drawn tight as a result of leaving campus when she should have stayed behind. At the time Barbara O'Malley suggested going to the movies, it had seemed like a good idea. They had all been working for nearly three weeks without a decent break, and Jennifer admitted she was getting a little stir crazy. Besides, all they had planned to do was take in a matinee and be back for dinner. The trouble was, no one had bothered to check the length of the film or when it began, so they had arrived an hour early, and the show had been well over two hours long.

She looked at her watch; it was just past five.

Lightning flared again, and she jumped, slapping a hand against the wall switch to turn on the lights.

Monsters, she thought again. Jen, what'll you think of next?

The room was small, but she didn't mind—it was just as comfortable as her room back home. To her left were the bed and nightstand against the wall, to her right a closet and an alcove with a low chest of drawers. Beyond that on the far wall a desk under the wide casement window, two armchairs she'd gotten from a Goodwill store downtown, and a rickety side table covered with piles of books. On the white walls were several posters framed in chrome—Sierra Club prints of animals and birds in the wild.

She liked to think of it as an efficiency apartment; she also considered it the one place she could escape to when she needed moments alone.

After stepping to the chest of drawers, she stared critically at herself in the mirror above it. Her head turned slowly from side to side, and her reflection returned her lopsided smile. Her hair was shoulder long and auburn, her face somewhat narrow but perfectly suited to the bright green eyes, the naturally dark lips, the slight tilt to her nose that made some think her English. She seldom worried about her weight—she was slender without half trying, and, despite her long legs, of average height.

A knock on the door turned her away from the mirror. When she called "Come on in," a girl poked her head in the room, and Jennifer grinned.

"I know, I know," she said, walking to her desk. "You lost your pen, right?"

Grace Korder smiled sheepishly. "I don't think they like me. They're always hiding or something."

Jennifer laughed. Grace was a plain, somewhat plump little girl who couldn't seem to hold on to anything—during the summer session's first week she had managed to misplace most of her books.

She found an extra pen in the drawer, tossed it across the room, and Grace snatched it out of the air. "Thanks."

"It's okay. I don't need it."

There was a moment's awkward silence before Grace smiled again, started to leave, and looked back. "Jenny, I . . . have you got a few minutes? There's something . . . I gotta talk to someone, Jen. I really do."

"I can't do it now," she said, puzzled. "I haven't eaten yet. You want to come with me?"

Grace blinked rapidly and pushed a nervous hand through her long, barely combed brown hair. "Uh, no. No, I can't. I mean, I've already . . . hey, look, I'll talk to you later, Jenny, all right?"

The door closed before she could say anything, and she walked back to the mirror, smiling thoughtfully. Poor Grace seemed to have at least two or three crises a day, usually about boys and getting along with the other girls. Though they weren't close friends, Jennifer felt a kinship with her because neither was the usual Thaler woman— very smart, rich, and on her way to getting richer.

Average, she thought as she took up a hairbrush, that was a fair word for her without putting herself down. Not a wallflower like Grace, but not likely to be a social whirl-wind either. Her parents had decided to send her to Thaler because they wanted nothing but the best for her, but at first they couldn't afford it. When she received the scholarship for her junior and senior high school years, her father was so happy he had bought what seemed like a hundred bottles of champagne and told anyone who would listen that his daughter would now be going to Harvard.

The enthusiasm didn't bother her. She might have to work just a bit harder than some, but books and their promises excited her. They gave her visions of worlds she had never seen, gave her imagination a chance to flex and grow.

Too strong, she thought with a quick smile, if I'm going to start seeing monsters just because I broke a school rule.

Lightning, much closer, and a rumble of thunder creeping over the hills.

She walked to the window and looked out through sheets of rain streaming down the panes.

Despite the gray haze she could see the Connecticut hills behind the campus still lushly green, the expanse of well-kept lawns that swept down a gentle slope to the playing fields and the gymnasium to her right and, though it was hidden by the dark and the trees, there was, far off to her left by itself in a patch of woodland, an unused, two-story building that had once been an all-purpose science lab until a new one had been built. Now it was deserted and off-limits to the students.

Someone knocked on the door.

She turned to call "come in," but looked back quickly when she thought she saw something moving out there. A dark flickering in a brief moment of startling blue white.

Something large.

Something that didn't look at all human.

Chapter Two

"HEY!" MONICA SAID, ENTERING THE ROOM WITH a grin and a laugh. "You going to stand there all night? I'm hungry!"

Jennifer didn't answer. She waited until the next flash, squinted, and saw nothing. It was a shadow, nothing more.

Nerves, she reminded herself. C'mon, Jen, it's just nerves.

"Jennifer!"

She took a deep breath and turned around.

"Dress," her friend ordered. "You want the guards to put us in solitary for being late?"

She laughed and danced out of the way when Monica lunged for a chair, threw herself down, and draped her legs over the arm, smoothing her white skirt over her knees. At Thaler the girls could wear what they liked on their own time, but in classes and at dinner jeans and slacks were forbidden.

"Dumb movie," Monica said.

"It wasn't bad."

Monica shook her head. "Jenny, isn't there anything in this world you don't like?"

"Brussels sprouts."

"That's not what I mean. You never have a bad word for anyone. Not even Marysue Beauford, for crying out loud."

"Oh, she isn't so terrible," Jennifer argued as she hurried into her skirt and blouse.

Monica groaned. "Oh Lawd," she said in a mimicking southern drawl, "Ah just don't know what Ah'd do without my smelling salts. Ah'd just die, Jenny child, Ah truly would."

Jennifer laughed. Marysue was as Monica had drawn her—a falsely fainthearted girl from a well-to-do Richmond family, who played the southern belle to the hilt, as if she were Scarlett O'Hara and Rhett Butler were waiting for her just around the comer. Monica, on the other hand, had no such immediate goal as a rich husband and hordes of children. As soon as she was done with Thaler, she wanted to head for New York and make her fortune in modeling, acting, or perhaps even television.

She was so ambitious that Jennifer often wondered how they had ever become friends. It wasn't that she didn't want a career for herself, but she was perfectly willing to take the years of college first, to study as much as she could so she'd know exactly what she wanted. Monica was impatient; she wanted it all now.

There was also the difference in their backgrounds: the Holts were old-money wealthy, while Jennifer's father had struggled all his life for what comforts they now had. Monica was stunningly beautiful, and Jennifer thought of herself as attractive but not spectacular. Monica had a devilish gleam in her eye from the moment she jumped out of bed; Jennifer, on the other hand, could barely bring herself to speak to anyone she didn't know. That she had begun to change she owed to Monica, who told her on the first day they'd met that the last thing she wanted in a place like Thaler was to be known as a bookworm.

"They'll torture you to death and scatter the ashes," Monica had warned, referring to a few of the more snobbish senior girls. "They'll drive you away, Jenny, if you don't at least hang out. Believe me, I know what I'm talking about. I've seen it before."

And she was right.

It had been painful at first, but Jennifer worked hard to overcome her reticence, and save for a few snide remarks about church mice trying to make it in the mansion, she was left alone.

"Girl, this isn't Prince Charming we're going to see, y'know," Monica chided with a grin. "It's only meat loaf and green peas."

"Okay, okay," she said, touching up her hair, smoothing down her blouse. "I just don't like to be sloppy, that's all."

"You ought to be a nurse."

"I don't like blood."

"You'd make a lousy vampire."

Jennifer turned violently, baring her teeth and hissing. Monica jumped, nearly falling from the chair, and scowled when Jennifer laughed.

"I'll get you for that, Field," she said as she headed for the door.

"I'll be ready, Holt," she answered with a growl and followed her around to the front, where they descended a wide, fan-shaped staircase into the foyer. She wasn't watching where she was going, and when Monica stopped abruptly she ran into her.

Filling the doorway was a tall, lean, dark-haired man staring at them grimly, hands clasped in front of him. He was dressed in a tailored black suit and a shirt so white it was almost blinding. His eyes were black and deeply set under equally black eyebrows; his hair was brushed away from his forehead to give him a vaguely satanic widow's peak; and his mouth was thin lipped and, now, tight with annoyance.

"Well, well," he said in a rasping deep voice, "I'm so glad you've returned."

"Returned, Mr. Dramon?" Monica asked innocently.

At that moment Marysue Beauford and Barbara O'Malley came giggling down the steps, and Jennifer heard Barbara say, "Oops," when they spotted the dean.

"And here are the others," Dramon said. He smiled without humor and slipped one hand into his jacket pocket. "Just the ladies I wanted to see."

They stood before him in a row, trying not to look at one another and not wanting to look into the man's eyes.

"You went to a film this afternoon," he said. "I assume, then, you've completed your studies?"

No one said anything.

"You understand, of course, that had an accident occurred, we would not have known about it." His free hand smoothed his tie, then pointed at their hearts. "We are responsible for you, young ladies, and while we cannot prevent you from leaving campus on your own time, we would appreciate it if you would let us know where you're going. We do have our obligations to your families, in case you have forgotten."

"Yes, sir," they muttered in unison.

"Very well, then." He stepped to one side. "You'll be late for dinner if you don't hurry."

They darted outside to the building-long porch, which had been added to that building and each of the others twenty years before. It wasn't until the door closed behind them that any of them realized they had forgotten their raincoats. Not that it mattered—none felt like facing Dean Dramon again.

Silently they hurried to their left, to a long covered walk that brought them to the adjoining building—the Student Union, which housed the dining hall, the bookstore, library, and health clinic. Rain lashed at their feet and spilled in waterfalls from clogged gutters. Farther ahead there were dim lights, white globes on black posts that led down the drive to the gates.

Other than that, the day was almost black.

At the door Monica stopped and looked back at Dramon watching them from the porch. Jennifer followed her gaze and couldn't help shuddering when he turned and walked off, a dark shadow in the storm's twilight.

"Are you afraid of him?" Monica asked.

"He's a spook," Jennifer said. "He gives me the creeps."

And as they walked into the welcome chatter and laughter of the dining hall, she shook her head and said, "Boy, I don't know how you've stood him all this time. He would have given me nightmares the first day."

Monica stopped. "Huh? What are you talking about?"

"Dramon," she said. "I don't know how you've made it for two years, with him sniffing around all the time."

'Two years?"

"Sure. You'll be a junior in September, right? So you've been here two years."

"Yeah, sure," Monica said. "But, Jennifer, until three weeks ago I never saw that guy in my life!"

Her room was damp even though the window was closed, and Jennifer hugged herself as she sat at her desk and watched the storm attack the hills. The wind had come up again, and it sped across the open ground to slam into the dorm, rattle the panes, and once in a while cause the desk lamp to flicker.

The light sweater caped over her shoulders did not ward off the chill, because the sight of the rain and the sound of the wind raised gooseflesh on her arms. She wished Monica were with her, just to talk, but soon after dinner her friend had vanished with Barbara, and she suspected they were involved in one of their card games—probably poker—down on the first floor.

And Grace had apparently found someone else to talk to—Jennifer hadn't seen her all night.

Down the hall she could hear a stereo blaring, words and music blurring to little more than raucous noise; someone raced past her door laughing, someone else followed with a shout; a radio came on to compete with the record.

She looked down at the book she was trying to study, found herself reading the same dull paragraph over and over again without remembering a thing, and closed it with a sigh.

Lightning filled the room with a harsh blue white glare.

Thunder ripped overhead.

She looked across the desk to the window and saw her face in the pane, ghostlike and pale and winking away whenever the lightning returned. With a shudder she turned her chair around to face the door and her bed. A yawn made her jaw crack, and she scolded herself for it; it was too early for sleep, yet the storm and the dorm's noise were making it impossible for her to work. Maybe she could go to the library, but the next thunderous blast changed her mind.

"You're being silly," she told herself, but just the same she couldn't help it. The room suddenly seemed very small, and she bolted to the door, opened it, and stepped into the hall.

The music had been turned down, but she could still hear it; there were shrieks from the shower room; and Marysue was leaning against the wall halfway down, combing her deep black hair and nodding as she listened to someone.

Jennifer moved on restlessly, down the stairs to the foyer.

One hand rubbed her arm absently as she turned to her left, looking through an arched doorway into the dorm's communal study. Here there were large desks and wooden chairs partitioned off into several cubicles, shelves on the walls for reference books, and a larger desk by the door where, on most nights, an instructor sat to help students until nine.

It was empty.

To her right, then, into the common room, fully thirty feet on a side, with comfortable chairs and couches arranged around low coffee tables. None were occupied now, making the room seem too large, too empty.

The ceiling-high windows whitened briefly with lightning, but the thunder that followed was distant and soft.

Still rubbing her arm, she wandered aimlessly, until she stopped in front of a large oil painting on the rear wall. It was a rendering of Thaler from the air.

Her eyes traced the road from the village of Staines to the massive marble pillars that flanked the school's main entrance. Beyond it, up a curving drive, were seven nearly identical buildings ranged along the outline of a crescent moon. Hers was the last on the left; then the Student Union, another dorm, administration, two class-room buildings, and a third dorm. Two of the dorms were closed for the summer session. Far to the right were three houses—one for the school's dean, the others for senior faculty. The rest of the teachers either had rooms in the dorms or rooms in town.

It was impressive. Over one hundred acres that had been an estate belonging to, depending on whom you listened to, either an oil pioneer or a Revolutionary War gun smuggler.

She frowned then and stepped closer.

Weird, she thought, squinting at the painting. The old science building. It wasn't there.

"Fascinating, isn't it?" a voice said softly, and she gasped and spun around, wondering why she should be feeling so guilty.

Peter Dramon stood in the middle of the room, hands in his pockets, his head cocked to one side; there was a faint smile on his lips. Beside him was a short, heavyset woman in a dark trench coat, holding a floppy-brimmed hat in one hand—Elizabeth Gantrel, head of the science department.

"I—I was just . . ." Jennifer gestured behind her toward the painting.

Dramon looked down at Mrs. Gantrel and smiled again. "I think," he said, "it's time we moved that old painting out, don't you, Mrs. Gantrel? Something a bit more cheery for this room. It's really not very well done. A curiosity, nothing more."

Mrs. Gantrel agreed with a grunt and a brusque nod that sent a wisp of graying dark hair over her creased brow. She swiped at it impatiently with a heavily ringed hand and shifted from side to side as if anxious to move on.

"Well, I guess I should go read or study or something," she said, nervously edging away from the painting. "I was just . . . the storm . . ."

"Please," Dramon said kindly, lifting a hand. "Don't leave on our account, Miss Field. We were simply making rounds to be sure everything's all right."

"All right?"

"Lightning strike," Mrs. Gantrel snapped as if Jennifer should have known. "Came down by the generator. Have you had any trouble?"

Jennifer shook her head. "The lights dimmed once or twice, that's all."

"Good," the woman said and slapped on her hat.

"And how are you doing, Miss Field?" Dramon asked as the three of them moved into the foyer, Jennifer scolding herself for acting as if they were going to attack her.

"Fine," she said with a weak smile.

"Your work, so I'm told, is more than just fine," he said gently. "Excellent and superior, I believe, are the words used in all the reports."

"Oh. Thank you."

Mrs. Gantrel had her hand on the doorknob, clearly impatient to leave.

"Thaler is very lucky to have you, Miss Field. Very lucky indeed."

Jennifer didn't know what to say. In the three weeks she had been there, Dean Dramon hadn't said more than a few sentences to her; now he was actually praising her as if she were some sort of rare genius.

He smiled, gave her a slight bow for a farewell, and left when Mrs. Gantrel opened the door. Jennifer started up the stairs, trying not to grin, but something made her turn when she was almost at the top.

Mrs. Gantrel was still down below, staring up and frowning.

Jennifer managed a smile.

Mrs. Gantrel nodded once and disappeared into the rain.

Chapter Three

"IT WAS REALLY SPOOKY," JENNIFER SAID. "SHE looked like she wanted to bury me alive or something."

Marysue Beauford laughed behind manicured fingers and shook her head. "You do think the oddest things, Jenny. My lord, the next thing you know you'll have us all murdered in our beds."

They were sitting in the hallway, a common sight once studies were done and room doors were open for visiting and gossip. Marysue was wearing a white shirt with the sleeves rolled above her elbows, the tails hanging out over jeans so tight Jennifer wondered how she could breathe.

"I didn't say that," she said. "It was just weird."

"Well, I think he's cute."

Cute isn't the word, Jennifer thought, as she pictured the dean as she'd seen him that night; Peter Dramon was one of the most handsome men she had ever seen in her life. But there was something about his face, the set of those dark eyes, that made her nervous and wary and unable to admire his looks. "Monica said he was new."

"Sure is." Marysue stared down at her bare feet, then picked up a bottle of nail polish and went to work; the color was so dark it was almost black. "Came around the end of July, I think."

"What happened to the old dean?"

"Who knows? Who cares?" She gnawed on her lower lip as she attacked another toe.

Jennifer leaned back against the wall and stared at the ceiling. "Marysue," she said, "can I ask you a question?"

"Sure, why not?"

"What are you doing here? In the summer, I mean. After all you've told me about your place in Virginia, all those horses and servants, I'd think you wouldn't want to leave."

"I'm studying, child, don't you know that?"

"But—" Marysue was not known for her superior grades, and it puzzled her that the girl should come all this way north just to attend a school she didn't like. Especially now, when there were barely two dozen girls and but a handful of teachers.

"Early outs," the girl said after studying her handiwork for a moment.

"Early outs?"

"Sure. You can graduate a year early if you take the right courses during these prison sessions." She looked up, and the innocent belle was gone, a calculating woman in her place. "I don't want to spend one more minute than I have to in this heap, you understand? I will have my diploma in June, Momma will be happy, and then I'm gone. I mean, Jenny, I am gone!"

Jennifer closed her eyes and hugged her knees loosely to her chest. "Funny," she said dreamily, "but sometimes I think I'd like to be a professional student."

"You are crazy, my dear."

"But there's so much to learn, Marysue! If I live to be a zillion, I won't have enough time."

"If you live to be a zillion, your brain'll be mush and you won't learn a thing."

Jennifer grinned, then giggled and nudged the girl's hand with her toe, causing her to paint a red stripe down the side of her foot.

"Field!" Marysue yelled.

Jennifer leaped to her feet and started running, Marysue right behind her, screaming threats of mutilation and murder as they ran past the shower room and pelted down the far corridor toward the front. Heads popped out of doors, a pillow was launched at Jennifer's head, and within moments it was apparent that an impromptu lynching party was at hand.

Jennifer ran on, amazed that she'd had the nerve to do such a thing, laughing so hard that her breath was soon gone, and she stumbled when she reached the central staircase. A moment later she was caught by a half-dozen girls who carried her back to the showers, arms pinned to her sides, her feet kicking uselessly. She screamed for mercy, but Marysue marched in front of the procession, fists brandished at the ceiling as she pushed open the swinging door and turned on the water in the first stall.

"No, Marysue, please, no!"

"You have defiled me, Jennifer Field," Marysue announced and nodded once, sharply.

Jennifer struggled futilely, but hands shoved her into the narrow tiled stall, and she gasped with shock as the cold water drenched her. When she recovered, she tried to drag some of them in with her, but they stayed just out of reach, laughing, until she reached up and turned the nozzle on them. They scattered instantly, loudly vowing revenge, and she slumped exhausted against the tiles for almost a full minute before she remembered to turn off the water.

Suddenly Marysue was back.

"Oh, please," Jennifer said, too weak to laugh, too weak to run again.

Marysue sneered, then tossed her a towel. "Get yourself dry, Field. You're a disgrace to your sex."

Jennifer dried herself off as best she could, then wrapped the towel around her shoulders and padded back to her room. A few girls still stood in the hall talking, giggling as she passed, cringing in mock fear when she scowled and muttered vengeance.

And when she was alone, her door closed, the storm rumbling gently over the hills, she felt a stinging in her eyes and brushed at it angrily. This was no time to cry, but she couldn't help it—this was the first time at Thaler that she felt accepted. The shower hadn't been a punishment, but a game; and the looks on their faces afterward were ones of promise, not malice.

It was a wonderful, almost giddy feeling, and after getting ready for bed, she stood at the window, grinning to herself and paying no attention to the shadows outside, shadows that moved even when the wind wasn't blowing.

The following morning was warm and bright; the only reminders of the storm were a few dead branches cast onto the damp grass by the wind, and an occasional shimmering puddle on the drive. At breakfast Jennifer and Monica were joined by Barbara O'Malley and her bulging backpack. Monica ate quickly, complaining about a field trip scheduled for that morning—a geological excursion into the neighboring hills. "Hunting the wild igneous rock," she said between bites of burned toast. "I'd rather do my laundry."

Barbara agreed, and Jennifer sympathized until, suddenly, she stared at them with suspicion. "Wait a minute. Isn't your geology class mixed?"

O'Malley dropped a fork, retrieved it, and dropped it again.

"That," Monica said, "has nothing to do with anything."

Jennifer grinned. "I think you two are protesting too much." She leaned over then and sniffed. "Perfume? For a climb up a mountain?"

"Field, you're a pain, you know that?" But she laughed when Jennifer didn't stop grinning. "All right, all right. There just may be a remote possibility of male companionship today. You happy now? But I believe I'm not the only one who has a class with townies." She looked at Barbara. "Boy townies, at that."

"No kidding?" Barbara said innocently, smoothing down her red hair. "I didn't know that. Boys? Really?"

"I believe so," Monica said.

They would have gone on if Jennifer hadn't waved them silent, shaking her head and wondering what O'Malley had stuffed into the backpack. Food, for sure; maybe some beer? Bathing suits in case they came across someplace where they could swim? But Barbara wasn't talking, and Monica ended the interrogation by sweeping everything onto her tray and marching out of the room.

Immediately outside the door, Monica grabbed her arm and sighed dramatically. "Oh, I think I'll die now and get it over with," she said in a loud whisper. "Heaven can't possibly be any better than this."

Across the brilliant green front lawn were dozens of kids standing in the shade of an ancient chestnut tree.

Most were girls, but a handful of boys hovered at the fringe. They were high school students from Staines, participating in the special summer session. A few of them, the brightest, also took the classes during the regular academic year. The stated purpose was to give the local youth college-prep courses before they graduated; the real reason was to keep peace with local authorities so that Thaler would feel no compunction about asking favors from them when the need arose.

One of the boys Jennifer knew very well—Lee Fawkes, a sandy-haired and lanky biology classmate.

Monica nudged her with an elbow. "He's looking this way, Field. Boy, is he ever built."

Jennifer scowled, not at the comment but at the warmth she felt rising from her neck. He was indeed looking at her, and now he was walking confidently across the grass toward them. Monica softly whistled, and suddenly decided she'd left an important piece of geology equipment back in the cafeteria. Before Jennifer could stop her, she was gone, and she could only wait until Lee reached her, his walk a slight swagger, a smile on his tanned face.

C'mon, she told herself as she smiled back. Act your age. But she couldn't help a touch of her hand to her hair, to the pale green shirt she wore hanging out of her jeans.

"Hey, Jenny," Lee said. "You on the field trip?"

She shook her head. "Rocks don't excite me," she said. "I can't see spending a whole day climbing a mountain so I know what wild granite looks like."

He laughed. "I thought you were interested in everything."

"I am, but—"

"Hi, Lee!" Monica said as she burst back out, her hands empty. "You going rock hunting?"

"Not me. I have to work."

Monica gave Jennifer an exaggerated wink and strode off toward the school bus waiting on the drive. She turned once and gave Jennifer the okay sigh with her left hand before laughing and breaking into a run.

Jennifer sighed silently. "You really have to work?" she said.

He hooked a thumb behind a wide leather belt. "Not work work, if that's what you mean." His father owned a local hardware store, and Lee usually filled in for vacationing employees. "Some of us aren't brains, y'know. We even have to study on weekends."

Jennifer said nothing. He never came on campus unless he absolutely had to.

"Not bad," he said then, watching Monica climb into the bus. "How come all of you rich people are so good-looking?"

She knew it was meant to be a compliment, but she resented the tone. It was obvious from his attitude that he was very independent, and more than a little resentful of the money Thaler represented.

"I'm not rich," she said stiffly. "I'm on a scholarship, just like you."

"Oh?" He looked at her with a grin. "But you think you're good-looking, huh?"

"That's not what I meant," she snapped.

"Don't worry about it," he said. "I didn't either."

She considered walking away then, or slamming her books over his head. Instead, they watched as Dean Dramon got onto the bus. Poor Monica, she thought. There goes all the fun.

"So," Lee said when the bus drove off and vanished between the marble pillars.

Jennifer smiled awkwardly.

"What are you doing today?" he asked.

"I don't know. Study, I guess."

"Study?" He backed away as if shocked. "On a day like this you're going to study? Books? Inside? At a desk?"

"You said you had to."

"That was before I realized what a great day it is."

She finally admitted she probably wouldn't work. What she really wanted to do was go for a walk in the woods.

"Man, that was close. For a minute I thought you were a bookworm or something."

"Only when I have to be," she admitted.

"So," he said again. And looked at the sky, the grass. "You going alone or what?"

She wanted to tell him she didn't feel like company, but knew it would be hard to tell him no without hurting his feelings.

And then she wondered why she cared—one minute he was arrogant, the next he was almost human. He was confusing. And it made her feel extremely uncomfortable.

"I thought you had to do something."

He shrugged. "It can wait." As though, if she asked him along, he'd be doing her a favor by agreeing to go.

A glance at the common, and she realized that taking a day off wouldn't kill her. Although it was true she had gone to the movies the day before, this was different. She didn't know why, but it was. And while she was astonished at her boldness, she didn't feel the least bit guilty when she led him to the dorm, asked him to wait on the porch while she changed her shoes, and ran up the stairs two at a time.

When the door closed behind her, she was out of breath.

"Jennifer Field," she said to her reflection in the dresser mirror, "what are you doing?"

She grinned as she rushed back outside, nodded to Lee, and they moved down the steps and around the side of the building, toward the woodland at the bottom of the slope.

The sun, without benefit of shade or breeze, was hot, and a haze of humidity clung to the distant hills. There were shouts from the playing field on the far side of the campus, and in one of the music rooms someone was practicing on a piano, badly.

At the tree line he guided her to the right, toward a worn path between two young oaks. As the ground leveled, they could hear the faint run of water directly ahead, and a scurrying in the branches that closed over them once they left the grass. The temperature dropped swiftly, and the cool air felt wonderful. It was a different world there, and she wondered if he spent much time in the woods, if he was a hunter, or if he just liked to walk.

She suspected that even if he did, he wouldn't admit it.

Lee crouched on the grassy bank, and she knelt with him, watching the water rush like molten glass over the rocks, seeing a glimmer of silver where fish darted out of the shallows and down the stream. A water spider skated across the surface. A jay called in the leaves above them.

She felt herself growing drowsy and reached down to cup some water in her palm and splash it lightly over her face. Lee did the same, then reached down and scooped a handful onto her arm.

"Hey!"

"Sorry. I missed."

"Missed what?"

"This." And a second scoop doused her cheeks.

She yelled and slapped water onto his legs, received the same in kind, and nearly tumbled in when she stretched out to deliver a deluge.

But she never did.

Suddenly from deep in the woods they heard a cry of pain. With an exchange of worried glances, they waded quickly across the stream and paused on the opposite bank, listening, until Lee jerked his head and they plunged into the trees.

They didn't hear the cry again.

"A joke?" she asked, not really believing it herself.

"I don't think so. C'mon."

"No, wait!" She took his arm to hold him back. "Maybe we ought to get someone . . ." And she waved vaguely behind her.

"If somebody's hurt, Jen, we haven't the time."

He plunged ahead, the trail gone now, forcing them to make their own path through the brush. Twice, he called out, but there was no response; Jennifer heard things and blamed them on her imagination. Finally, they reached a small clearing filled with wild flowers and surrounded by white birch.

"Oh, no," Lee said hoarsely.

Jennifer could only stand there, staring in disbelief at the body of a young girl lying in the grass.

Chapter Four

SEVERAL SECONDS PASSED BEFORE EITHER OF them could move. Then Jennifer rushed forward and dropped to the ground beside the motionless girl, who was dressed in a pale blue western shirt and faded jeans that looked as if someone had taken a razor to the bottoms; her feet were bare and bleeding slightly at the ankles; her hands scratched and smudged with dirt. Her long hair was tangled, wet strands of it webbed across a soft round face.

"Do you know her?" Lee asked, standing to look anxiously at the woods around them.

She swallowed hard. "It's Grace," she whispered as she reached out a trembling hand to touch the girl's cheek. "Grace Korder. She's—she's from out west someplace."

There was no blood that she could see, but her heart nearly paused when she realized the girl wasn't breathing. She fumbled for the girl's pulse, found none, and placed her ear against the chest. Nothing. Not a sound, not a beat.

Oh, no, she thought, rocking back to her heels. Oh, no, she can't be. Just last night she wanted to—

"We need help," Lee said decisively. "We have to get someone, the nurse, a doctor—"

"Go!" Jennifer said sharply. "Hurry!"

"What? I didn't mean me. You—"

"For goodness sake, Lee, there's no time. Go!"

She had no idea what made her do it, what made her send him away, and she regretted it as soon as she heard him crashing back toward the stream. She turned on her knees to call to him, to tell him not to leave her alone with the body, but nothing passed her lips. Her throat was dry, her breath hot and labored.

Suppose, she thought suddenly, there's someone here, someone who . . . she scanned the trees wildly, one hand at her throat, listening intently for the sound of someone, or something, coming toward her. A killer. A murderer. A beast of the woods that shouldn't be there.

She remembered the figure she thought she'd seen during the storm.

And before she could stop herself, the trees became menacing and dark, the birds grew claws, the animals long fangs that dripped with fresh blood.

Stop it! she ordered.

Suppose there was a gang of them. Suppose Grace had been kidnapped or something, and in making her escape had been—

Jennifer, will you please stop it!

She closed her eyes tightly, until a sudden welling of nausea was stifled; then she turned back and stared down.

There was no murderer coming after her; there were no monsters in the Connecticut hills. She was alone and would remain that way until Lee returned with help.

Another look at the body, and she bit hard on her lower lip. She had no training beyond elementary first aid, but she had no doubts that the girl was dead. It was a sensation more than anything, a feeling that life had slipped away, and she began to tremble, shake, and she scrambled away to the clearing's edge. There were tears, and she brushed them away with the backs of her hands; acid rose to her mouth, and she swallowed heavily. And when she was able to look back, she couldn't resist moving closer.

There was something odd.

Something wrong.

There was no blood, no marks beyond the scratches caused by flight through the underbrush, no sign at all that she had been assaulted in any way.

Then Jennifer saw it and blinked rapidly.

The girl's lips, the tips of her fingers, widening blotches across her cheeks, even the toes and the sides of her feet—they were slowly turning blue.

Impossible, she thought after she checked again; she looks like she's been suffocated, but how can that happen in the middle of the woods?

An obstruction in the throat.

No, she decided; she'd still be struggling, choking, trying to cough it up. What she and Lee had heard had not been the sound of someone strangling.

Her brow creased. She stretched out a hand and touched an arm, drew it back as if it had been burned— the flesh was cold, icy cold, and that was wrong too.

And for a brief moment she thought of Grace wanting to talk to her, worried about something and afraid to tell her when other people were around.

Oh, no, she thought. Oh, no, what if—

The faint noise of people coming through the trees distracted her, and she turned her head slowly, her mind gone abruptly numb, her limbs refusing to obey when she tried to stand as Lee burst into the clearing, Miss Hoburn, the school nurse, close behind, followed by the tall stooped figure of Briggs, the custodian.

Lee immediately put his arms around her shoulders and lifted her to her feet, held her tightly while the nurse made a swift examination of the body, muttering to herself and shaking her head. When she was finished, she directed the bald-headed man to carry Grace back to the clinic. Then she walked over to Jennifer, her white uniform and whiter hair a charged contrast to the woodland's soft green.

"Are you all right, dear?" she asked quietly.

Jennifer managed to nod shakily.

"Young man, take her back to the infirmary, please. I think a mild sedative is in order."

Lee didn't argue, but Jennifer called out as the nurse hurried after Briggs. The woman looked over her shoulder, a penciled eyebrow raised.

"Grace. Is she . . .?"

"I'm afraid so, dear. Now hurry, young man. This is neither the place nor the time for questions."

Jennifer wanted to know what had happened, but Lee's strong arms propelled her forward. She protested that she was all right, but as soon as he released her, her knees weakened again and she almost fell. Dizziness forced her to cling to his waist, and it wasn't until they reached the stream that she was able to walk on her own, without feeling as if her legs would desert her.

When she pulled away, she saw him reach for her and change his mind, and she had the impression he was actually embarrassed by the concern he had shown her.

By the time they were halfway back, Miss Hoburn was gone, and Lee was several yards ahead. She called to him to wait, and told herself it wasn't the time to lose her temper when he looked over his shoulder, scowled, and shrugged as if he didn't care. Despite him, she caught up. Slowly.

She hurried, every few steps breaking into a trot and slowing again.

"Jenny, take it easy!" Lee told her. "You're gonna break a stupid leg."

"I'm all right," she insisted. "Really. I'm . . ."

Tears once more filled her eyes, and she turned her face away as they fell. She barely knew Grace, but the manner of her dying, and her age, and Jennifer's own reaction to it, were too much. She wept and did not try to stop until they were out of the trees and angling toward the back entrance of the Student Union.

"Jenny."

Her hand reached out and closed around his. "I'm sorry." Then she looked into his face and saw the pain in his eyes, and the fear. "What about you? Are you okay?"

"I'll live. It's just . . ."

"I know."

And they said no more, communicating only with an occasional squeeze of hands until they were inside and walking down a pale green corridor to the infirmary door. Once inside, in the small, brightly painted reception area, Jennifer dropped into an uncomfortable, molded plastic chair, Lee beside her. An open door led to the examination room, and by leaning forward she could see the padded table and Grace's body on top of it, covered with a sheet. Someone was talking on the telephone, probably to the police.

"It's a good thing she was there," Lee whispered.

Jennifer gave up trying to eavesdrop on the conversation and looked around. "She? Who?"

"Miss Hoburn. She was standing right behind the dorm when I got out. That's why I was so quick getting back." His right hand combed roughly through his hair.

"Boy, suppose she'd gone on that trip. We'd have to deal with the cops ourselves."

The murmuring in the other room stopped. Briggs lumbered out and into the hall, not looking at the two sitting nervously by the door. A moment later the nurse appeared, shaking tablets from an unmarked bottle.

"How are you feeling, Miss Field?" she asked.

"All right, I guess. Miss Hoburn, what about—"

"Good, good. That's fine." She held out her hand, and Jennifer took the pills offered. "These are sedatives, for your nerves. I want you to go straight to your room, take two now and two when you go to bed tonight." She nodded once, sharply. "Mr. Fawkes, I can't give you any medication, but I suggest you go right home to your family. Would you mind taking Miss Field back to her dorm first?"

Lee shook his head.

"Excellent."

"Miss Hoburn," Jennifer said insistently. "Miss Hoburn, what about Grace?"

The nurse stared at her. "What about her?"

"I mean, how . . . what happened?"

"I'm not prepared to say at the moment," the woman replied after a slight pause. "That's for the doctors at the hospital to decide." A glance at Jennifer's wide eyes, however, made her smile briefly. "I'm sorry, Miss Field. I don't mean to sound like such a dragon. But you'll have to admit, something like this doesn't happen here every day."

She nodded sadly.

Miss Hoburn's smile returned. "Were you a good friend?"

Jennifer admitted she wasn't.

The woman nodded. "I see. But you want to make sure there's not a killer roaming around the woods, right?"

"Yes," she said and grabbed for Lee's hand.

"Well, on that score, I can ease your mind. You obviously didn't know that Grace had epilepsy, and she'd been told over and over again not to traipse through those woods alone. I'm sorry to say, it looks to me as if her illness finally caught up with her."

Jennifer looked at the floor and said nothing.

"Mr. Fawkes, if you don't mind . . .?"

Lee, muttering a word of thanks, tugged gently on Jennifer's hand until she stood, then led her to the hall where, after a look to the swinging doors of the dining hall at the other end, he brought her outside. And once there, he took a long, shuddering breath he released explosively. Jennifer followed his example, and the fresh air, though hot, tasted sweet indeed.

"C'mon," he said gruffly. "I'll walk you back."

She didn't want to go. She didn't want to be left alone in her room, the image of Grace's body floating ghostlike through her mind. And as if he sensed that, he walked slowly, rubbing the back of his neck. At the dorm entrance they sat on the porch's top step.

The common room was empty.

There were no sounds from anywhere, not even the trees that hid the wall.

"I've never seen a dead body before," he said at last, his voice sounding far younger than his years. "Not really."

"Neither have I," she said. "How horrible for her. To have to live with something like that."

"Yeah."

She shifted a bit closer. "I was so scared out there."

"You sure didn't act it," he said, admiration in his tone. "You were great. You knew just what to do. It wasn't your fault she was . . . it was too late."

"I don't feel that," she said glumly. "I keep thinking there must have been something I could have done. If we had been a little quicker, maybe, or hadn't stopped to play stupid games in the water, maybe we could have reached her in time to help." She looked hard into his eyes. "We might have been able to save her, Lee. We might have."

He shook his head. "No, I don't think so."

"But—"

"But nothing," he said. "We didn't know she was out there. Like Hoburn said, she had no business going there on her own. We didn't know, and we couldn't have known." He waited, and when there was no response, he squeezed her hand. "We're not magicians, y'know. We're not responsible for things like that."

She nodded reluctantly. "I know you're right. But I still feel lousy."

"No kidding. So do I."

They sat for another fifteen minutes, not feeling the sun, not hearing a flock of crows squabbling in the trees. Then Lee finally rose and reminded her of the nurse's order.

Then he looked at her sideways. "You, uh, mind if I give you a call later? To see how you are, I mean."

"No," she said. "What about you?"

"Me?" For a moment he seemed to resent the question, then sniffed and gave her a one-sided grin. "Hey, I'm fine. No problem."

Jennifer smiled at his concern, then thought in sudden panic, He's going to kiss me. Oh, no, he's going to kiss me!

But he only touched her shoulder and hurried off the porch, though not before she saw a faint reddening of his cheeks. She watched as he settled into a comfortable trot that led him toward the gates, watched a moment longer in case he decided to return, then headed inside and slowly climbed to the second floor.

The rooms were empty.

The only sound was her breathing.

From her dresser she grabbed a plastic glass that she took into the bathroom, filled, and grimaced as she swallowed the first dosage the nurse had given her.

After staring in the mirror, she glanced down at her watch.

It had been more than thirty minutes since Briggs had brought Grace's body back to the infirmary, twenty, at least, since she heard Miss Hoburn calling the police.

But no one had arrived.

Not even an ambulance.

Chapter Five

JENNIFER TURNED AWAY FROM THE MIRROR, intending to return to the nurse's office and find out why there'd been no response to Miss Hoburn's call. Though Staines was a small town, it did have a hospital, and the emergency squads weren't so overworked that at least one coulvdn't have come right away. Something must be wrong.

But the moment she stepped into the hall she felt a slight blow on the back of her head, and her knees began to buckle. With a startled gasp she leaned against the doorjamb, one hand to the back of her neck.

"What . . .?"

It was a long second before she realized that no one had hit her, that the surprisingly abrupt sensation had come from inside. Her head felt as if it were spinning to the gentle rush of a damp warm wind, and her mouth felt as though someone had packed it with dry sand. It frightened her into gasping again and biting back the urge to cry out. Then she closed her eyes and waited for the puzzling spell to pass, opened them again and winced at the sudden impenetrable glare of sunlight flooding the floor, driving off all color until everything was white.

"Oh, no," she muttered and clamped one arm over her stomach.

Instantly her mind conjured an image of Grace, lying blue and dead in the clearing, and she feared the same thing was happening to her. But the terrifying notion passed quickly. Her breathing steadied. It was the medicine, that was all. Whatever the nurse had given her was working already, but producing a reaction neither of them expected.

It should only have made her sleepy; it shouldn't be dropping her into the middle of a nightmare.

But it *was* the medicine, nothing more. And now she had to get out of there before something more happened. Her room, then. She had to get to her room and lie down. When the reaction was over, then she would make her way to the infirmary.

A nod brought on a rush of dizziness, and she pushed away from the door, turning and moving slowly along the wall, her right shoulder giving her support, her left hand out to give her balance. Her stomach lurched, and she paused, taking slow, deep breaths until the danger of retching had passed. The light intensified, bringing tears to her eyes she didn't dare brush away for fear of falling.

Holding a doorknob grimly, she peered through the white light curtain to her room at the hall's far end.

"Oh, no," she said. "Oh, no, I'll never make it."

It seemed a hundred miles away, and when she began moving again, her door receded from her, making her stumble along a continuously lengthening tunnel that soon tilted up and away, then down like a steep slide that, if she fell, would take her into the black depths of an endless cave.

"Help," she whispered.

But there was no one to hear her.

"Lee," she whispered.

But he was gone. They were all gone, and she was alone.

From the shower room behind her she could hear the thunder of a dripping faucet; from below, the can-nonfire of the common room's air conditioner fighting against the day's heat.

Her eyelids felt weighted; the muscles in her arms slowly grew rigid, sparking with faint pain; and she deliberately grunted aloud with each shuffling, awkward step, as though the sound were a counterspell that would prevent her from collapsing before she reached her goal.

Step, and grunt, and the tunnel stayed the same.

Behind her there was a muted roaring, a beast stalking her trail.

At one point she knew she was going to fall, that she wouldn't be able to take another step, move another inch.

They were going to come back and find her lying in the hall.

"No!" she told herself and kept on, pressing harder against the wall, ordering her legs not to stop. The bed was just up there, waiting for her. Soft. Comfortable. Warm and ready to take her to her dreams.

It seemed like hours before she finally realized she was standing in front of her door, staring at it as if she'd never seen it before. She sobbed and closed her eyes briefly, opened them again when she was assaulted by spears of blinding white. Turning the knob was painful, pushing the door inward was a major accomplishment. But she was in, and she was turning, spinning, dropping onto the mattress.

Where she slept.

And saw the figure of Peter Dramon striding swiftly and silently across campus toward her, dressed in black that did not reflect the sun, wearing a long black cloak with a vivid red lining, his face pale save for the crimson slash of his lips, his eyes deep and black and staring straight at her.

Jenny

She didn't want to answer, somehow knew it would be a fatal error, and turned away, only to see Elizabeth Gantrel crouched and waiting on the porch roof, dressed in raw furs that gave her the look of a gray she-wolf on the prowl, sharp teeth exposed, nostrils flared, her eyes deep and black and staring right at her.

Jenny?

She whirled to the right, to run around the side of the dorm and into the safety of the trees at the bottom of the slope, had taken only five steps when Lee and Marysue appeared shimmering in front of her, hand in hand, their faces in shadow though the sun was burning, their feet bare and ending in claws, their clothes more fur than cloth, and their eyes in a sudden flare deep and black and staring straight at her.

Jenny!

A turn—Dramon was less than five feet away.

A turn—Gantrel was springing at her from the roof.

A turn—Lee and Marysue were running toward her, hands outstretched, blue black claws glinting and sharp.

She screamed.

"Jenny!"

And opened her eyes.

And saw Monica kneeling on the floor beside her bed, hands on her shoulders to prevent her from leaping off the mattress and running away.

"Jenny, are you all right?"

A sob broke before she could stop it, and she shook her head vigorously to dispel the last of the nightmare. Then a careful scan of the room, and all the familiar things slowly moved into focus.

"Wow," Monica said, concern fighting with relief in her expression. "That must have been a champ." She leaned back, sat, and crossed her legs. "You sure you're all right?" A hand darted behind her to close the door.

Jennifer nodded. "I think so." With one sleeve she wiped perspiration from her cheeks and felt a momentary chill shudder through her legs. "Powerful medicine Hoburn gave me. It almost knocked me out before—" She stopped. "Monica, do you know—"

Monica nodded. "Yeah. I almost croaked when I heard it." Then she grimaced and slapped her cheek lightly. "Lousy choice of words."

Still trying to drive the nightmare away, Jennifer pushed herself up until she was sitting back against the wall, her pillow bunched in the small of her back. "I found her," she said in a small voice.

"I know. We heard."

There was a knock on the door, and when she nodded, Monica reached up and opened it. Marysue was outside, frowning, a brush in one hand and a glass of water in the other. Jennifer accepted the glass gratefully, suffered another round of explaining why she had screamed, then sighed as the Virginian slumped into an armchair.

"I swear I didn't think there are that many cops and ambulances in all of Staines," Monica said.

"What?" Jennifer said.

"Sure. Didn't you . . . no, of course not. You were in outer space."

"Was I really a wolf? Funny, I always thought of myself as a bird of paradise," said Marysue.

In spite of herself, Jennifer smiled.

"Must have been three cop cars and four ambulances," Monica said in amazement. "Seems someone got the word wrong, and they thought the whole place was burning down. Fire engines, the whole works. Dramon nearly had a coronary, and I thought Gantrel was going to sue the whole country for something or other." She smiled. "I don't think Miss Irongut Hoburn is long for her job."

Jennifer suddenly felt weary, and when she choked on nothing, she asked Marysue for another glass of water. And when Beauford was gone, she said, "Monica, have you talked to Lee?"

"That gorgeous creature? Not since this morning, why?"

"What time is it?"

"About four-thirty."

"That means I've been out the whole day! He was supposed to call, to see if . . . to see if I was all right."

"Well, m'dear, he hasn't called once." A quick laugh filled the room. "Lord, don't tell me you've fallen for that hunk? Not that I wouldn't mind checking him out myself, but—"

"It isn't anything like that," she said more sharply than she'd intended, and Monica's hands flew up to show her she was only kidding. Explanations had to wait when Marysue returned, followed by what seemed to be half the dorm looking for gossip and offering sympathies.

No one mentioned Grace.

Jennifer assumed it was because they were too shaken by the girl's death and didn't want their friends to know how affected they were. When they finally realized, however, that she was no longer participating, one by one they drifted out, making plans for dinner and afterward, telling her that if she needed anything all she had to do was call.

Monica was the last to go.

"You gonna be okay, Field?"

"Yes. Thanks."

"No problem. I'm starving, though, so I'm heading down to the dining hall. You ought to come, y'know, even for just a salad."

"Maybe later," she said, swinging her legs over the side of the bed. "I'm still a little shaky."

"Sure thing. And if Lee calls, I'll take care of him myself. After all," she said, "what are friends for?"

Jennifer grinned as Monica left the room, and then looked out the window toward the hazed hilltops. She supposed that the comedy of errors produced by the nurse's phone call should have made her laugh outright, but she could not shake the feeling that there was something odd about that morning's events. Nothing that couldn't be explained, she was sure, but like a terrier with a bone, she was unable to let go once it had taken hold in her mind.

Twenty minutes later, after washing her face and changing her clothes, she wandered weakly down to the dining hall, ate sparsely and alone, and checked the oversized bulletin board in the Student Union foyer for word of a memorial service or a suspension of classes because of Grace. Nothing special, however, had been posted. Only the usual notices of class meeting changes, people selling clothes and musical instruments and books and even a car, reminders of excursions, reminders of tests.

Not a word about Grace that she could see at all.

And when she stepped outside again, she wondered why Lee hadn't gotten in touch with her.

Her mood became glum. Probably, she thought, he didn't want to get involved any more than he was already. All that talk about worrying about her was just that— talk. Nothing more.

Suddenly the idea of returning to the dorm was depressing, and she decided to walk awhile to clear her head, maybe find a ball game she could join or someone to talk to. Anything was better than returning to her room, where she knew the nightmare was waiting to take her again.

She walked blindly, kicking idly at the grass, picking up a length of dead branch and whipping it at the cooling evening air. The trilling song of a finch caught her attention, and she listened with a smile until it faded and was lost; a glimpse of a rabbit in the trees by the wall made her want to chase after it, to find its burrow, to see if it had a litter that season. For a while she stood at the pillared entrance to the campus, looking down the winding, hilly road toward Staines, hoping she might see Lee on his way back to visit her. It was empty, however, save for the occasional passing car, a hawk circling lazily overhead, a pair of crows strutting boldly across the tarmac.

"You're wasting your time, lady," she muttered. "All he cares about is using the academy to get what he wants. And you are definitely not it."

With a resigned shrug she returned to her room where she changed into a dark shirt and jeans. Then she went out again and wandered until she found herself near the trail she and Lee had taken earlier.

She didn't want to go in and follow it.

There was nothing to find there.

But with a slow turn of her head, she mentally retraced the route they had taken on their walk, trying to pinpoint the direction of Grace's cry. Along the trail, to the stream, and the frantic plunge through the brush to the discovery in the clearing. And when she thought she had located it, knowing it was only pure guesswork, she knew she was looking toward the half-ivied walls of the abandoned science building.

Now that, she told herself, is silly. Do it again, kid, you've made a mistake.

Because of the way Grace was facing, she had to have come from that direction. And the distance would have been about right. It had to have been from near the old building.

Wrong, Field, wrong. Nobody, but nobody goes near there anymore. It's too dangerous. The place is falling down. There are snakes, for heaven's sake.

Another step.

She wished Lee were with her, or Monica, or Barbara; even Marysue would be welcome company right then.

The sun was still up, but she felt as though she were walking through midnight and jumped when she caught a glimpse of her shadow keeping pace beside her.

"Enough," she said. "Go back, you dope."

And screamed when someone put a hand on her arm.

Chapter Six

"HEY!" SAID LEE, JUMPING BACK WITH HIS HANDS up to avoid a wild swing from Jennifer's arms. "Hey, Jenny, it's me!"

Her panic subsided when she recognized him, replaced by a surge of irrational anger, and the temptation to demand to know what he thought he was doing, sneaking up on her like that and scaring her half to death. Abruptly, she felt awfully foolish and offered him a sheepish smile.

He grinned back, shaking his head. "Hey, if I'd known I had that effect on you, I'd have worn a mask or something."

She giggled, not because the remark was funny, but because she was relieved. "Frankenstein would fit, I think."

"Thanks a lot. I'll do the same for you someday." He walked up to her again, looked over her shoulder, and a frown crossed his face. "You weren't going back in there, were you?"

She shrugged. "Maybe." And turned to face the trees.

"That's crazy," he said. "Forget it."

"Maybe," she said again.

He managed a short, apologetic laugh. "Hey, look, I'm sorry I didn't call. Dad had to hear the story forty times before he'd believe me. Then I had to stack cartons."

And then they were quiet and looking at the dark-ening trees as the sun touched the top of the distant hills. As they watched, she told him of her reaction to the sedative, how frightened she had been, and how intense her nightmare had been. He sympathized and slipped an arm around her waist, hugged her briefly, and released her as if embarrassed.

"But I still can't figure it," she said with a frown. "I mean, it just doesn't feel right."

"But Hoburn—"

"Look, I know what she said," Jennifer snapped. She crossed her arms over her stomach, then brushed her hair back with one hand. Suddenly she made a loud gagging noise, fingers clutching at her throat, one hand waving wildly over her head as she staggered backward. Her eyes widened, her mouth gaped for air, and Lee was too stunned to do anything but stare.

And as suddenly as it had begun, the pretend attack ended and Jennifer said, "Does that sound anything like we heard today?"

He blinked. "Jenny, I thought you were . . ."

"Were what?" she asked quickly.

"I don't know. Strangling. Choking."

She nodded once.

He spread his arms in confusion, then held up a hand. "Oh, no," he said. "No."

"Hoburn told us Grace had epilepsy, that she probably choked to death." She closed the distance between them and grabbed his hands tightly. "But that wasn't what we heard, Lee! Grace wasn't choking at all! She screamed."

"So? Maybe she felt the attack coming. She knew she wasn't supposed to be out there on her own. She was probably scared."

A glance toward the buildings, a stare at the windows to see if anyone was watching.

"How long did it take us to reach her?"

"Not long," he admitted after a second's thought.

"Long enough for someone to suffocate?"

"No," he said quickly and scowled. "But she had all the signs, right? She suffocated, we saw it."

"We both saw a body that looked like it had," she reminded him. "She was already dead when we got there."

Lee pulled his hands free from her grip and stuffed them into his pockets, looked up at the sky and squinted. "It . . ." He shook his head once and took several steps toward the trees before kicking at the ground lightly. "What are you trying to say? That she was killed? Murdered?"

"I don't know," she said truthfully. "I really don't. It just doesn't make any sense, that's all."

He looked over his shoulder. "You have a great imagination."

"Grace wasn't my imagination."

He lowered his head in thought, and she waited for him to say something. None of it had occurred to her before then; the idea had grown around her sense of something out of place, and now that it was in the open, she wanted to talk herself out of it, to believe that it really was only her imagination. But the more she thought about it, the more she knew she was right.

And the colder she became.

Lee mumbled something to himself.

A sideways look to the dorm nearly blinded her when the sun struck the back windows and speared light into her eyes.

"The cops," he said then, so quietly she could barely hear him.

"They've already come, Monica told me."

"At the hospital, they'll know. They'll have to—they'll know if something happened to her."

"Then we'll go there," she said.

His laugh was sarcastic. "How? Fly? And say what—'Excuse me, doc, but could we sit in on the autopsy? We were friends of Grace, and we want to see how she was murdered.'" A hand gestured in disgust. "C'mon, Jenny, be realistic."

Frustrated at his reasonableness, she wanted to shake him until he agreed to do what she wanted. The trouble was, she didn't know what that was. He was right about the hospital, the nurse, even the police. And so, why did she still feel as if it were all slightly out of focus, that there was something lingering at the corners of her vision, something she couldn't quite pin down because every time she turned her head, it vanished.

"Jen?" He was standing in front of her, ill-at-ease and unhappy for it. "Look, I can't stay long, okay?"

She nodded wearily. "It's all right. Maybe I'm still fuzzed with that sedative."

"Yeah," he said eagerly. "That's probably it."

It wasn't. And she didn't want to go back to the dorm where he had left his bike. But she did because she couldn't think of anything else to do.

The bicycle, a rusted and somewhat battered racer, was lying on the grass by the porch steps. When she saw it, and saw the trouble he had getting it erect, she grinned in spite of the foreboding that whispered darkly to her.

"This is how you got out here?"

"My trusty steed," he said, as if daring her to make something of it. "Never fails me more than four or five times a week."

She almost asked him why he didn't get a new one, or a car, and knew the answer immediately—he couldn't afford it.

Her ill humor faded; she put a hand on his arm.

"You okay now?" he asked.

"Sure," she said, not quite a lie.

"Listen," he said, not meeting her gaze. "You'd better not say anything to anyone about what we were talking about, okay? I mean, you ought to sleep on it, Jen. You did have that nightmare, and you sure don't know what kinds of things that drug's done to your head." He paused. "What I mean is, don't get all hysterical over nothing. We're not doctors. We don't know a lot of things. Just sleep on it, maybe it'll all make sense in the morning."

The urge to argue was strong, but she fought it down; once again, he was making maddening sense.

Then he peered down the drive. "Tomorrow's Sunday."

"Right."

"The store is closed on Sunday."

She hid a smile behind a hand, looked to her left and saw Monica standing just inside the doorway. "Right. And there aren't any classes either."

"I don't think it'll rain, do you?"

"Oh, for heaven's sake, Lee," she said, unable to contain her delight any longer. "If you come out around noon, maybe we can do something, okay?"

His smile was broad, and before she could say goodbye, he leaned over and kissed her lightly before pedaling away. Amazed, and not displeased, she watched him speed around the arc of the drive, and didn't hear Monica until she was right behind her.

"Field, you are incredible."

"He is, isn't he," she said dreamily.

"Not him, jerk. You. Now move it. We're going to be late."

"Late?" She let herself be dragged up to the porch and along the covered walk toward the Student Union. "Late for what?"

"Dramon wants to talk to us," Monica said grimly. "About our responsibilities to the school, to each other, and to ourselves."

"How do you know that?"

"It's what deans always do when there's trouble."

"Oh." She slowed. "It's because of Grace, right?"

Monica nodded. "He put the word out just a few minutes ago."

Jennifer wasn't sure she was up to listening to a lecture that was sure to make her feel more guilty than she already did, but there was no getting away. But she did manage to find a place in the back of the dining hall, and as the dean droned on about Grace, her mind began to drift, and she began thinking about Lee's admonition to put it all into perspective and keep the hysteria out.

Suddenly a sharp elbow in her side brought her back, made her look blankly at Barbara, who was staring at her oddly.

"Hey, you asleep or what?" the redhead asked.

"Of course not."

"Then maybe we should go." O'Malley grinned abruptly.

Jennifer looked around and realized the room was virtually empty. She laughed in embarrassment as the others grabbed her arms and practically carried her outside. Once there, however, she sobered and watched the dean as he headed toward his house.

Monica sidled up to her. "Hey, you thinking about that hunk of yours?"

She shook her head.

Marysue stood in front of her. "Do you need help? Is that crap old Irongut gave you coming back on you or something?"

She shook her head again.

Barbara threw up her hands and walked off in disgust, saying pointedly she had better things to do than watch one of them turn into a stupid zombie. The others remained, however, until she finally stirred, checked behind them to be sure they were alone, and asked what they'd heard about Grace Korder's death; but before either of them could react, she headed for the side of the Union, beckoning them to follow.

"A mystery," Marysue said gleefully. "And I thought this place was too dull to be real."

"Beauford," said Monica, "you are something else, you know that? You are really something else."

"Why, thank you, dear."

Monica glared at her, then turned the glare on Jennifer when they were out of sight of anyone else. "All right, Field, give, huh? What's this all about?"

After a deep breath to calm herself, and after a second's debate over the wisdom of saying anything at all, Jennifer told them. As much as she could. Thinking that hearing someone else besides Lee tell her she was making something out of nothing would let her get back to those things which were important—her studies.

And true to form, Marysue scoffed from almost the first word; Monica, on the other hand, was fascinated. She didn't believe a word of it, she said when the story was over, but she suggested they check out the clearing right away, if only to put Jennifer's mind at rest.

"And what would that prove?" Marysue asked scornfully.

"I thought you wanted a mystery."

"A mystery, yes. Not a dumb thing like this."

Jennifer almost wept. Arguing wasn't what she wanted at all.

"Well, if you still insist on this nonsense," Marysue said finally, with a hard look to the sky, "I've got a flashlight in my room. I'll get it and be right back. In case you hadn't noticed, Holt, it is getting dark in them thar woods."

"I noticed, I noticed," Monica said. Then, when Marysue was gone: "Jenny, this is crazy, you know that, right?"

She nodded.

"And you know I'm doing this just to prove to you that you're out of your gourd."

She nodded again and smiled.

"All right, then. Just so you know."

They waited.

The sun drifted below the hills, and the campus swam with shadows.

"Monica, what if I'm right?"

"Don't say that, Jenny. You're not."

"But what if I am?"

"Then we are all going to be in serious trouble."

Chapter Seven

AFTER MARYSUE RETURNED, JENNIFER HESITATED only once, at the start of the path, before taking a deep breath and plunging into the woods without a backward glance.

The shadows darkened swiftly under the trees, gathering in pools and low walls that made the footing treacherous, and twice she stumbled over tangled roots protruding from the grass.

The first stars began to appear, pale and distant.

Nightbirds began to stir.

Rustlings in the brush sounded louder than they were.

Distance and time were distorted, and Jennifer was surprised when she stumbled at last into the clearing. The others crowded up behind her, and she pointed, saying nothing—there was still enough light to see the crushed grass where Grace's body had lain.

The wind picked up, and for a moment they could hear the faint sound of music drifting over the campus; then it shifted, and there was silence.

And owl hooted directly overhead.

Jennifer angled to her left, peering at the brush for signs of Grace's breaking through. After a few seconds' searching she found it—a laurel bush with several broken branches, its green leaves scattered on the ground.

With a grunt of satisfaction, she stared into the trees, squinting to see through the twilight that had fallen there. Then she nodded toward the broken bush and the woods beyond. The others looked at her fearfully, but she wasn't going to stop then. With a prayer that they would follow, she plunged into the woods.

Luckily, the going was easy. The underbrush was not thick, and Grace in her panicked flight for help must have stumbled into everything large and small that grew under the trees. On one thorned branch they found a piece of her shirt; beneath another was a shred of ribbon. And it wasn't long before they ignored the signs because they knew exactly where they were headed.

Twenty minutes later, they reached it.

It loomed out of the trees, dark chipped brick and gray fieldstone, its arched windows boarded over with sheets of plywood, brittle weeds and ivy crowding darkly around its foundation. The old science building was two stories high, and despite the forest's creeping in to swallow it, there was still a band of clear ground completely surrounding it.

There was a silence there that unnerved them. None of the nightbirds could be heard, and the wind that brushed across the crowns of the trees made little more than a soft hissing sound. When a twig snapped underfoot, it was as loud as a gunshot.

As one, they stepped back, staring up at the second floor, then moved toward the front entrance, a tall single door made of metal. It was recessed in the wall, and it was locked.

Jennifer rapped on it with her knuckles. Then a second time, harder; it was solid and unyielding.

They studied the front again before moving to the far corner and peering around it. After an exchange of glances, they made a complete circuit of the structure, finding no open window, no other door. When they returned to the front, Jennifer was disappointed.

And relieved.

She had obeyed her instincts, and they had proven her wrong; at least now she'd be able to sleep.

Marysue studied the building again, frowning, and said, "I wonder when this thing was built."

And Jennifer remembered the picture in the dorm's lounge.

The science building wasn't in it.

She scowled as she recalled someone's telling her the picture had been done only a few years before for the academy's centennial. Yet this place had obviously been here for quite some time. And if it were part of the Thaler campus, why hadn't it been included in the painting? Because it had been abandoned?

She looked more closely at the stone, the bricks, and wished she knew more about how things like this aged.

A better question was—why had it been given up? It looked sound enough, and it certainly wasn't the collapsing derelict she had been led to believe. There was no debris for anyone to turn an ankle or break a leg on, no pits or holes in the ground, and no sign at all that anyone had ever tried to force a way in. Surely, she thought further, at least some of the locals would have made the attempt—for simple curiosity, if nothing else.

Why then, she wondered, aren't we supposed to be here?

"Field," said Monica lightly, with a tap to her arm, "are you still on this planet?"

Jennifer looked at her oddly, but before she could explain what she had been thinking, Marysue said, "Someone's coming!"

At first no one moved.

The wind picked up, the leaves rustled loudly, and shadows swept in waves across the face of the building.

Jennifer tilted her head as if it would help her hearing, but it was Beauford who grabbed her arm again and pointed.

"Over there," she whispered. "Someone's heading this way."

They ran immediately to the safety of the trees and dropped behind a low wall of brambles when it was obvious they would make too much noise if they kept on going.

"We're gonna get killed," Monica whispered, and Marysue hushed her angrily.

Twilight became dusk, and the old deserted building was as difficult to see as if they were looking through a thin black veil. Shadows filled the clearing, stars filled the sky, and the first hint of the moon began to rise above the forest.

They waited, not moving, barely breathing.

Finally, Jennifer nodded in the direction of the campus.

A faint white light suddenly appeared among the trunks in the distance, bobbing, vanishing, reappearing as someone approached along a winding path none of them had seen. Whoever it was moved slowly, obviously in no hurry, and Jennifer relaxed just a little, glad that at least they hadn't been spotted or heard.

The building seemed to grow as the dark crept in. A large cloud of gnats spun and whirled toward their faces, and Jennifer batted them away impatiently, spitting when she thought one had landed on her lips. The owl sounded again; a nighthawk screed softly overhead as it hunted for its evening meal.

The temperature dropped.

When Marysue shifted, a twig snapped under her heel, and they all tensed, ready to run in case they were discovered.

The light broke from the trees, white and blinding, making it impossible for them to see who was carrying it. They ducked when the broad beam swung in their direction, held their breath and raised themselves slowly when it swept over the windows, as if checking to be sure everything was still intact.

Then it focused on the door.

Jennifer gaped at the dark figure behind it.

"Damn, it's Gantrel," Marysue said. "What's she doing here?"

Jennifer shrugged, watching intently as the woman made her way to the door. There was no hesitation, not a hint of unease; she moved with the confidence of one who had done this countless times before without interruption. Even the casual way she held the flashlight told Jennifer the woman felt perfectly secure.

She was wearing a light coat that reached almost to her ankles, and her hair was covered by a dark green scarf. Her face was in shadow as light bled from the sky, but there was something about the outline Jennifer didn't understand. It was clearly Mrs. Gantrel—her manner of walking, her size and shape pointed to it—but the shadows shifted too wildly as the flashlight bounced around, too wildly for her to see what bothered her.

"That's it, I'm outta here," Holt declared quietly. "This girl does not want her little butt kicked out of school."

Jennifer turned to dissuade her, but Monica was already creeping back through the trees, making so little noise Jennifer had to blink to be sure she could still see her outline.

"What?" Marysue whispered.

"She's gone."

"Creep." A pause as the flashlight scanned the grounds again before aiming at the door. "You game to see what's going on?"

Jennifer looked at the building, looked back in the direction Holt had taken, and almost told her she was going to go back too. Monica was right—this was hardly the way to end a scholastic career, and certainly no way to start one, not when she was so dependent on scholarships from the academy.

Then Gantrel, after pulling up her collar and giving a final glance around, tucked the flashlight under her arm, fumbled in her pocket, and pulled out a large iron key. She held it close to her eyes, nodded once, and unlocked the door. A look at the boarded windows of the second floor, and a stabbing with her light, and the woman was gone without a sound.

Inside.

The door closed silently behind her.

"Well?" Marysue said.

"I don't know."

"Well, make up your mind. I don't want to camp out, y'know."

Jennifer's grin was one-sided, but she had noticed there had been no problem with the lock; it had opened smoothly, which meant it was not stiff or rusted from disuse. And she couldn't take her eyes away from the splinters of light behind the plywood window coverings, marking Gantrel's progress through the building to what, she guessed, was a corner room. The light steadied, grew brighter, and changed to faint gold; the woman had turned on a lamp.

"Well?" Marysue asked eagerly. "We going to take root, go back, or what?"

"Or what," Jennifer said decisively. And before her nerves deserted her, she crawled around the bramble wall and rushed across the ground in a half crouch, Marysue right behind her.

Half expecting someone to shout at them and pin them down with a spotlight, they came up against the side wall toward the back, pressing against it and looking over their heads to a window just above. They heard nothing, but the wood had come away from its mooring just enough so that one of them might be able to peer inside.

Marysue seemed to read her mind and told her to go ahead.

Jennifer closed her eyes and crossed her fingers, praying that when she looked, she would see nothing more sinister than a secret hideaway, a furnished room where the woman could escape the constant chatter and the noise the students spread over the campus, and find a little peace, a place to regroup before going back to the wars. Or, better yet, she thought, a cozy little nest where she met secretly with her lover and shared bottles of rare wine and romantic music.

She almost laughed aloud—Mrs. Gantrel and a lover?

Marysue jabbed her, telling to get on with it before the sun came up.

A nod, and she puffed her cheeks, turned, and slowly raised herself up to the gap between stone and wood. Marysue kept one hand in the middle of her back.

At first the light was too bright, and Jennifer couldn't see a thing. Then her vision adjusted, and she blinked in astonishment, looked down at Beauford, looked back and swallowed.

This was no love nest, and it was no place to find a moment of peace.

The room was large, apparently running the full width of the building from the front to the back. From her awkward vantage point, she could see a number of long lab tables covered with white cloths, here and there stained with blotches of green and pale yellow; on the far wall opposite the window was a roughly made worktable above which had been set a series of shallow metal shelves holding dozens of beakers, vials, and small cartons, many of them unopened. By pressing hard against the stone, she could see down to her right at a similar arrangement on the near wall.

The most curious thing, however, was something she was only able to catch a glimpse of no matter how she wriggled to improve her angle of vision. It was down at the back, in a space all its own, no tables or shelves anywhere near it. It was difficult to make out details because it was just beyond the reach of the light, but when she squinted she thought it was large, and oval, and it glinted like embers wherever its facets glowed.

And it was, as far as she could tell, at least ten feet high.

Her fingers began to ache from digging into the stone, and she lowered herself, leaning heavily against the wall while Marysue took her place. Visions of Frankenstein and his monster, Dr. Jekyll and Mr. Hyde and every mad scientist film she had ever seen flashed through her mind.

A laboratory.

Marysue dropped beside her then, and they looked at each other in puzzlement. It was frustrating not being able to talk, but Jennifer wouldn't have known what to say anyway. Answering this one question had only produced a hundred more, and she was no closer to her peace of mind than she had been when she'd started.

Marysue tugged at her arm, jerked her head, and they made their way to the next window, hoping to find one they could look through in order to see the machine, or whatever it was, more closely. Once Jennifer stumbled over a loose brick that had fallen from the eaves, and they froze in the moonlight, waiting for Mrs. Gantrel's cry of discovery. Holding their breath. Looking worriedly at each other. Finally getting to their feet and examining the plywood coverings as best they could without using their flashlight.

But their luck had run out. The windows were solidly sealed, set deep into the frames without a hope of a loose comer.

With frantic hand signals, Marysue suggested strongly they get out of there and go home. Jennifer was tempted, but she was also more curious than ever and wanted to have one last look inside. When Marysue made a face, she stuck out her tongue with a grin and headed back, paying no attention to the hand that plucked at her shirt.

At the window she lifted a finger, a promise she would only look once and quickly, and then they could go. After wiping her hands on her jeans, she lifted herself up again and waited until she was able to see as she had before.

Things had changed. The light was somewhat brighter, and there was activity inside.

She heard a low humming.

Something bubbling over a fire.

A sudden rush of frigid air seeped through the gap and made her shiver.

Then Mrs. Gantrel stepped into her line of sight, and reached up to take the scarf from her head.

Jennifer couldn't help it—she gasped aloud.

Gantrel whirled around, stared, then ran for the door.

Jennifer grabbed Marysue's arm and sprinted frantically for the trees, not saying anything, ignoring her friend's unspoken questions as she charged into the woods. They ran with the aid of Marysue's flashlight, keeping it pointed at the ground as they tried to retrace their steps back to the clearing.

She had no idea how long it took, could only hear her own footsteps, and imagined Gantrel closing the gap.

Then the clearing at last, and she stopped, held her stomach and gulped for air. Marysue, knowing only that they had been spotted, tried to get her to move on, but Jennifer balked, looking back over her shoulder constantly, listening for running footsteps.

She heard nothing.

The woods were silent.

"What did you see?" Marysue asked then, and when Jennifer told her, the blood drained from her face. "You're kidding, right?"

"No. I wish I was."

"A trick of the light. It had to be."

Jennifer nodded the possibility.

It had to be; otherwise, Mrs. Gantrel's hand was covered with fur.

Chapter Eight

BARBARA LOUNGED WITH ONE SHOULDER AGAINST the door, her right hand holding a vivid pink bathrobe closed over her stomach, her left constantly toying with stray curls of her red hair. Monica was slouched in an armchair, still dressed and holding a cigarette whose smoke she blew out the open window. Marysue and Jennifer were on the bed, legs up, backs against the wall. No one else had been allowed in; and as if in retaliation, every stereo in the dorm was going full blast, each with a different album.

"No," Jennifer was saying for the fourth time, "I can't swear to it, I told you that. Like Marysue says, it could have been a trick of the light. But it sure looked like it to me."

"Boy, that's gross," Barbara said. "Maybe she has a terrible disease or something." She shuddered and pulled the robe more snugly across her chest.

"Some disease," Marysue scoffed. "It's turning her hairy, like a man."

"She's practically one already," Monica said with a laugh as she threw the cigarette into the night air, shrugging when Barbara glared a reprimand at her. "A little more hair won't make any difference."

"That's not right, Monica," the redhead said. "If she's sick, maybe she doesn't want anyone to know about it."

"I don't think she's all that sick. Maybe in the head, but that's about it." She clapped her hands once and laughed. "Hey, I know what it is—advanced lycan-thropy."

Barbara frowned her puzzlement.

"It means," Marysue said patiently, "that you're a werewolf."

"Oh," the redhead said. Then she stared at a lock of her hair and scowled. "Oh, right. Sure she is. And when the moon is full, I'm Dracula's daughter."

"No, no," Monica said in disgust. "That's not what it means at all. Someone who has lycanthropy thinks he's a wolf, or that he can turn into a wolf. He doesn't really. He just thinks he can, that's all."

Jennifer giggled, knowing it was only nerves, yet unable to do anything about it. The idea of Elizabeth Gantrel turning into Lon Chaney, Jr. and killing peasants was ridiculous, despite the sudden memory of the fever dream she'd had.

"They kill people. Tear 'em up. Drink their blood, stuff like that."

Barbara's face paled. "Really? That's a real thing? You think that's what Gantrel has?"

"No, I don't," Monica said. "I don't even think she has fur on her hands." She held up a hand to stop an interruption. "I know what Jenny saw. I know what Jenny *thinks* she saw, anyway. But it could have been a hundred things—a glove, a shadow, part of her coat . . . I don't think that's the important thing, anyway."

"Yeah," Barbara agreed with a quick nod. "The thing is, did she see you?"

Jennifer shook her head after a look at Marysue, who dismissed the idea with a wave of her hand. "I don't think so. She knows someone was out there because I made a noise, but at most she could only see my eye."

"And a very distinctive one it is, Field," Monica said, making a clumsy monocle with two fingers and peering at her through it. "A very important clue, Watson. Very significant. Of course, she'll have to put us all behind a hole in a wall before she can spot who it was."

"Holt, will you knock it off?" Marysue said.

"Why? This whole thing is silly. You guys are blowing it all out of proportion."

"I didn't run away," Beauford said.

"You don't get any medals for that, lady. I was smart. I didn't get caught, did I?"

"No one did."

"Forget it," Jennifer interrupted before the argument grew heated. "She didn't see me, okay? She didn't see either of us. The important thing now is that lab down there."

"Oh, yeah," Barbara said, remembering, but still looking dubiously at Monica.

"Something," Jennifer continued, "is going on there, and they don't want us to know about it. All summer we got stories about how dangerous that place is, and it's in perfect shape! That means a secret. And when Grace's trail led us there . . ."

"Now wait a minute!" Barbara and Monica said at the same time. They exchanged glances, and Monica nodded. "Are you saying that Grace was . . . that Grace was murdered because of what she found out?" the redhead asked skeptically.

Jennifer shrugged, but Marysue wasn't so reluctant.

"It sounds like that to me," she said. "I mean, what other explanation is there?"

"The right one, you jerk," Monica declared heatedly. "If you'd only stop running off at the mouth, you'd know what it was. She had epilepsy, just like Hoburn told

Jenny. Maybe she did see something, but the attack was brought on because she was running away, not because they zapped her with a laser or something. Will you guys ever grow up?"

"Or maybe," Marysue said as if Monica hadn't spoken, "they used her in some awful experiment and she got away." She shuddered. "My lord, suppose that's it?"

"That's it, all right," Barbara said, opening the door behind her. "I don't want to hear any more of this. You are all out of your minds, and I don't want to be here when they come to take you away."

"Hey, Barb," Monica said.

"No! I don't want to hear it. I don't want to know it. I just want to—"

And the door slammed, the noise from the hall abruptly cut off.

They were silent for a long time.

Jennifer brushed at her knees, her shirt, then looked at the window, at the reflection of the room against the black of the starless night. Clouds had moved in over the past hour, and though there were no rumblings of thunder, she could feel them as if the dorm itself were stirring to life.

"A government grant of some kind," Marysue suggested, her voice startling the others. "Defense Department projects, things like that. They're always getting schools to do their dirty work."

"Thaler?" Monica said derisively. "You've got to be kidding."

"Why not? It's perfect, when you think about it. There are only about twenty or thirty of us here, right? And we're too busy with our studies and hiding from Dramon to get in their way. And they sure did a good job of keeping us out of the place. Until now. Why not?"

It almost made sense, but Jennifer did not join in Monica's argument against the notion; it would be fruitless. If Marysue had said the sky was blue on a perfectly sunny day, Monica would automatically take the opposite side. What she needed was not the bickering, but a calm discussion of what to do next. She was still of two minds about Grace, but she did not dismiss the possibility that somehow, whatever was going on in that lab had something to do with her death.

But what was going on?

She was not a stranger to a laboratory set-up, yet, except for the tables and assortment of glassware, nothing looked familiar. She ought to have seen something she recognized.

With a worried frown, she pushed herself stiffly across the mattress and stood up, gingerly massaging the small of her back and staring at the door without seeing a thing. Any moment now, she thought with a shudder, Mrs. Gantrel was going to come charging in with the dean right behind her, screaming about trespass and vandalism and generally raising hell, the result of which would be her immediate dismissal and a return home in disgrace. And she couldn't have that. It would kill her parents; it would ruin any chance she had of getting into college; and it would separate her from all her new friends.

". . . Hoburn," Marysue said.

She turned, tying to focus on what her friends were saying. "What?"

"I think we ought to ask Hoburn," Beauford repeated. "Why not? She's not as bad as the others, right? You could go down there, tell her you had a reaction to the medicine she gave you before—which you did, so it's no lie—and could you have something a little milder. Then, in a very clever way, you could see if she knows about the lab." She spread her hands and grinned. "Simple."

"Yes, you are," Monica said. "That's dumb."

Marysue jammed her hands on her hips. "Y'know, Holt, you've been a pain in the butt ever since this afternoon. What's the matter with your head? Don't you want to know what they're hiding down there?"

"Not really," Monica said, speaking mostly to Jennifer. "But only because I don't think it's any of our business what Thaler does with its property, and because I don't want any of us kicked out of here for something stupid like this."

Jennifer looked at Monica and tried to tell herself the girl really was concerned, and probably quite frightened as well. But so was she. In fact, she was scared to death. But if something was going on, if Grace actually had been killed for knowing what it was, they had to find out, and find out soon. If only to protect themselves.

Grace may not have been the only one in danger.

At last Jennifer said, "But it won't hurt to ask. If Hoburn doesn't know anything, she won't be any the wiser."

"You can't go at night," Marysue said.

"Why not? She's always in the infirmary or in her room. Either way I'll find her. If you're worried, you guys can always save me."

She pulled open the door before either of them could stop her and paused only a moment before hurrying to the steps. When she reached the foyer, she glanced into the common room to see if anyone was there, glanced into the study area and saw the lights all out. No one had followed her, and as she reached for the doorknob, she wished at least one of them would—to give her moral support, if nothing else, or to talk her out of doing something stupid.

Music blared down the staircase.

She sighed and went outside, turned left and hurried to the Student Union. She told herself there was nothing to worry about, that Gantrel hadn't seen a thing and probably, by now, had decided it was only an animal trying to get in. Nevertheless, she could not stop herself from looking across the commons at the shadows cast by the lamps, at the dark line of the wall down by the road.

She prayed that Lee would come riding up on his bike.

She slowed, hoping that Monica would chase after her, drag her back to the room, and tell her what a dope she was being.

If all that she speculated on were true, why hadn't the police returned? Surely someone at the hospital would want to know what had triggered Grace's attack.

She went into the Union and down the corridor toward the infirmary. The dining room and the game room were dark, and when she passed through the swinging double doors that separated the office from the rest of the building, only every other recessed ceiling light was glowing, adding length to the hallway, and making her heels sound like the crack of a whip.

Unconsciously, she rose up on her toes.

She drifted to the wall and let her fingers skate along it.

And when she reached the infirmary, she stopped.

She shaded her eyes and tried to peer through the door's translucent top half, but she could see nothing except the glow of a tiny lamp far in the back.

Go back, she ordered herself then. It's closed, you can't see Hoburn. Obviously she's off duty, as she should be on Saturday night.

But her hand closed around the cold brass doorknob.

The doorknob turned.

She closed her eyes, held her breath, and slipped inside, dropping immediately into a crouch as she hurried across the room. She barked a shin against a table, and she groaned as she grabbed for it, massaged it, stumbled sideways and nearly collided with the wall.

You'd make a rotten crook, she told herself; you'd get killed just turning on the stupid light.

The small lamp in the back made her pause.

The door to the examination room was closed and locked when she tried it.

That's it, she thought. Game's over, go home.

But she moved swiftly to her left, to the framed counter where the receptionist sat, and after a brief hesitation, swung herself up and over, wincing when her foot struck a covered typewriter, which she grabbed for frantically before it slid off the desk. Then she hurried to the other door that led to the examination room. This door wasn't bolted against her.

She opened it cautiously, ready to run in case someone shouted, then ducked quickly inside, closed the door, and leaned against it.

Something was on the padded table, its form hidden under a stiff white sheet.

The lamp dimmed.

Back, she told herself. Don't be a jerk, go back.

She took a step forward.

Another step told her it was a person under the sheet, head half-covered.

Oh, no, she thought, but without pausing, without stopping to think about what she was doing, she pulled the sheet away.

The scream that she knew had been waiting in her throat all this time started to move up, gagging her, making her back away while her hands waved denials in the dark air.

The body on the table belonged to Amanda Hoburn, and in the dim light she could swear the woman wasn't breathing.

Chapter Nine

SHE HAD NO IDEA HOW SHE MADE IT BACK TO her room without awakening the entire campus.

One moment she was standing terrified in the infirmary, the next she was racing along the covered walk. There was no memory of leaving the office or the Student Union, only a whirl of dark shapes and dim lights that seemed to follow her and spin away whenever she looked back.

There was no sound she could hear beyond the thunderous pounding of her heart, which made her chest ache, and the rasping of her breath that filled her lungs with flaring embers.

The moon was high, but the light it gave was veiled by wisps of clouds that trailed over its face.

Shadows stalked her.

Something flew overhead, small and black and swift in the night.

A gust of damp wind nearly knocked her off her feet.

As she charged onto the dorm's porch, she collided with something in the dark, spun away and kept on running; she expected to be grabbed at any moment by someone standing silently in the long shadows that covered the lawn, or at the building's far corner, or there, lurking by the door, tall and evil and dressed entirely in black.

But nothing, no one, stepped into her path, and she burst into the foyer with a muffled cry of relief and took the stairs two at a time, using the walls to propel herself sobbing to her room.

Once inside, she slammed the door shut and leaned heavily against it, eyes closed and head back, trying to calm herself and, at the same time, tell herself that something had to be done, now, before anyone else died.

Her knees buckled then, and she slipped to the floor in the dark, hands over her face.

Her lungs burned, her throat felt raw, and no matter how hard she tried she could not think straight.

Images like shadow plays flew across her mind—Miss Hoburn on the table, Grace in the woods, Mrs. Gantrel lifting a fur-covered hand and with a smile springing out a set of gleaming black claws.

Ten minutes passed, and she began to hear the noises of the dorm; another ten minutes, and she pulled herself to her feet and switched on the light.

The room seemed perfectly normal, exactly as she had left it only a few minutes before. Her books, the mirror, the faint odor of Monica's cigarette, the fragrance of Marysue's perfume.

It's not a dream, she told herself; it's not a dream, I'm wide awake; and she took a series of long, deep breaths and blew them out loudly until her hands stopped trembling and her legs lost the feeling of being filled with ice.

Quickly then, she brushed her clothes into some semblance of order and opened the door, intent on finding either Monica or Marysue to tell her what she'd seen, and to demand to know why they hadn't waited for her.

A single step over the threshold, and Jennifer saw Marysue down the hall. Jennifer waited patiently for her friend, leaning against the jamb and not smiling.

"Well?" Marysue asked, looking around to see if anyone was listening. "Tell me, Sherlock, c'mon!"

"Where's Monica?"

Beauford grimaced and pushed Jennifer gently back into the room, though she left the door open a crack. "She . . . we sort of didn't agree after you left."

"Marysue—"

"She said I was a jerk for letting you go, and I said she was a bigger jerk for not—" She stopped, looked, and put her hands on Jennifer's shoulder. "Jenny, what's the matter?"

"Miss Hoburn," she whispered, felt her knees growing weak again, and sat on the edge of the bed.

"What about her? What did she say?"

"I saw her . . . she was in the infirmary and she . . ." Tears filled her eyes, and she rubbed them away angrily. "She's dead."

"What?"

"She's dead. I saw her on the examination table. She's—"

"Jennifer, what are you talking about?"

Jennifer grabbed the girl's hands and yanked her down beside her, stared into her eyes and couldn't believe it when she saw pity in them, and a slight touch of fear.

"Marysue, you've got to believe me." And she explained as rapidly as she could what she had done, and what she had found. "We've got to get to the police. I mean, we can't let it—"

"Jenny, no."

". . . go on. First Grace, then Miss Hoburn. Marysue, we're right! Something's happening, and someone is killing—"

"Jenny, no," Marysue repeated forcefully. "You're wrong."

She stopped, released the girl's hands, and shook her head. "What do you mean? Marysue, listen, I know what I saw. And—"

Marysue looked as if she were about to cry. "Jenny, Miss Hoburn isn't dead." And it was Marysue's turn to hold hands, firmly, as she leaned forward and forced Jennifer to look at her. "She can't be dead, because Barb just came back from seeing her."

"No." She shook her head insistently. "No, that's impossible. I *saw* her!"

"Barbara cut her leg shaving," Marysue said, softly. "She took a really gross slice from her leg. You must have just missed her on the way back. She went over to the infirmary—"

"No. No, Marysue."

"—and Miss Hoburn patched her up. If you want, I'll drag her out of bed. She's really playing it up. You ought to see it. I think she thinks she should have a wheelchair or something."

Jennifer stopped listening. Instead, she tried to remember every step of the way over, every move she made to get into Hoburn's office, everything she saw or heard until she found the body on the table. Acid churned in her stomach. The tears returned, and this time she didn't stop them.

Marysue hugged her.

"It's all right, child," she said, her Virginia accent deepening. "It's all right."

"I wasn't dreaming," Jennifer insisted against the girl's shoulder. "I know what I saw."

"You know what you thought you saw," Marysue corrected without raising her voice. "It was dark, right?"

"There was a light."

"Not a bright one."

"No," she admitted reluctantly.

"And you were scared. She was probably just taking a nap. You know, sometimes I think she sleeps half the day. And you thought—"

Jennifer broke away and strode to the dresser, grabbed a tissue and blew her nose, grabbed another and wiped her eyes.

"Do you want me to get Barb?"

She shook her head. "It's hard," she said at last, walking now to the window and hugging herself. "I know you're not lying, but when I saw her there on the table, I would have sworn she was dead. I guess I'm more upset than I thought." A look over her shoulder. "I'm not crazy, you know, if that's what you're thinking."

"I'm not thinking that," Marysue said almost angrily. "I am thinking, though, that maybe all that garbage she gave you today hasn't cleared out yet."

Maybe, she thought. But it was all so *real*.

The door pushed open, and Monica stood there, frowning. "I heard somebody say crazy," she said. She was wearing a black nightshirt with an eagle emblazoned across the chest, and her blond hair was messy. "You weren't talking about me, right?"

Jennifer stared at her, then shook her head as she decided not to say anything about what she'd seen. What she didn't need then was a lecture, however well intentioned, and a demand she stop pursuing an illusion. She did, however, say that she'd had a scare, and Marysue attributed it to a delayed reaction to the sedatives.

Monica nodded. "Sounds like classic Hoburn," she said. "Sometimes that woman is totally brainless. You ought to see what she did to O'Malley's leg. She must have done it in her sleep, for crying out loud."

There was an awkward silence, because Marysue wouldn't look at Holt, and Monica wouldn't look anywhere but at Jennifer.

"Well," Jennifer said, too brightly, too falsely. "I'm tired, you know? I think . . . I think I'll get some sleep."

"Good idea," said Marysue. "And don't bother with breakfast. It's Sunday, remember? Powdered eggs and phony pancakes." She looked down at herself, sighed in mock distress, and shook her head sadly. "I swear, ladies, I am going to waste away to purely nothing before I leave this place. Maybe I could get my father to sue. Malnutrition or something like that."

Jennifer smiled and laughed quickly when she caught Monica examining her own figure. Monica scowled and mumbled something about the children they let into this place these days. Marysue winked and, after a questioning look, left as well.

Don't think, Jennifer ordered herself then. Don't think about anything.

She undressed, threw on a robe and padded down the hall to take a shower. Keeping her mind a deliberate blank while the hot water rinsed away the sour odor of fear. Afterward, while she was towel drying her hair, Barbara stepped out of one of the shower stalls, greeted her, and hobbled out, the bandage on her shin bulging as if she'd had minor surgery.

Jennifer sagged against the sink, head lowered, then roused herself with a sigh and headed back for her room. As she reached for the doorknob, Monica tapped her on the shoulder.

"Hey, you okay?"

She nodded. "Yes. Just tired, I think."

Monica looked at her worriedly. "Jenny, I don't know about you sometimes, I really don't."

She wanted to drop it, not to get into another argument, but she couldn't help one last attempt. "I saw the lab, you know. That much, at least, wasn't my imagination."

"I believe you."

"And you saw the trail Grace left. She came from that building, or"—she added before Monica could interrupt—"from that direction. I'm sorry, but I just can't help wondering."

"I know." Then she lowered her voice. "I hate to admit it, Field, but I couldn't sleep because I've been thinking about it."

Jennifer almost collapsed with relief in her arms.

"But don't get the idea I think there's something screwy going on, okay?" the girl said hastily. "I'm just curious, that's all."

"Then maybe we could find out something tomorrow, huh? Lee said he might come around and—"

"Lee?" Monica leaned back. "Lee, as in Lee Fawkes?"

"Sure."

"Jenny, it's really none of my business, but I think we're pretty good friends, right? And I think maybe you shouldn't be hanging around that guy too much."

Jennifer was puzzled. "Why? You think he's going to attack me or something?"

Monica gave her a look of disgust. "Don't be stupid. But he's not really . . . I mean, he's kind of weird, you know?"

Jennifer couldn't resist a smile. "You seem to think he's worth looking at."

"Looking at and hanging out with are two different things. He's not one of us, you know what I mean?"

"No," she said coldly. "No, I don't know."

Monica reached out to touch her but brought her arm back and rubbed the hand over her side. "He doesn't like us, Jenny. He thinks we're snobs, and all he wants is what he can get out of us, without giving anything back." She paused, then said with a rush, "I think he only pays attention to you because he thinks he can get you to fall for him."

Jennifer felt a swell of anger rise in her throat. "Is that so bad?"

"Of course!" Monica said. "Because then he can dump you."

"That's doesn't make sense. Look, I'm tired. I'm going to bed, okay? I'll see you in the morning."

She stepped into her room, had the door half closed when Monica stopped it with a hand. "Jenny, I'm not trying to move in, you have to believe that. But you're so damned sweet, sometimes you think everyone is as nice as you."

"Okay. Now—"

Monica dropped her hand. "I don't want you to get hurt, Jen, that's all. I just don't want you to get hurt."

Jennifer closed the door slowly, the anger giving way to a feeling of shame for doubting her friend's intentions. As always, she was only trying to make life smoother for her, and Jennifer knew she should be grateful.

But there was something about Lee, something in his gruffness that attracted her. She didn't know why, because he'd certainly given her enough cause to send him on his way. But maybe Monica was right. Maybe she ought to be more careful. Just in case. Just in case Lee wasn't all that he seemed.

Lord, she thought, you really are a mess.

She brushed her hair, dressed for bed, and stood at her desk, composing herself so that when she crawled under the sheets, she'd not lie awake all night, thinking. A finger tapped the cover of a book, and when she finally looked down, she saw it was last year's yearbook, one Monica had lent her so she'd know something more about the school.

Something tugged feebly at the back of her mind as she opened it, stared blindly at the first page, and closed it again; something was trying to work its way into thought, but as soon as she concentrated, it faded and was gone.

She shrugged. If it was important, she'd remember; if it wasn't, she wouldn't have to worry.

A yawn so long and loud that it made her laugh. She switched off the light and climbed into bed.

The dorm was silent.

The wind had come up again and was testing her window.

And as the day finally took its toll and exhaustion pulled her at last into sleep, she thought she heard Mrs. Gantrel's voice whispering in the hall.

Chapter Ten

THE FOLLOWING DAY JENNIFER AWOKE WITH A groan. Her head felt as if it had been thumped all night with a rubber hammer, and a look at the sheets twisted around her legs showed her what a bad time she'd had. She didn't remember any dreams. Nor, when she stared at the night table, did she remember hitting the alarm clock. It was lying on its side, and when she tipped it upright, she gasped when she realized it was almost noon.

At first she was annoyed that no one had tried to get her up, then sheepish as she realized they were only trying to help. A good long sleep, they must have decided, was the best thing for her. And maybe it had been. But it certainly hadn't done anything for her head.

She groaned again and sat up, grabbed her robe and made it down to the bathroom and back without seeing a soul, without hearing a thing. By the time she was dressed, her headache had faded, and a glance out the window showed a bright but overcast day. The clouds touched the air with a hint of damp, yet oddly made no promises of rain.

Her stomach growled.

Rubbing her eyes as she took the stairs down, she decided she'd have to apologize to Marysue for acting so crazy about Miss Hoburn and to Monica for snapping at her—although, she thought, the girl had no right to talk about Lee that way. Especially when it was she who had warned Jennifer about the so-called snobs when she'd first arrived on campus.

Maybe, she thought as she stepped outside, good old Monica is a little jealous.

The idea was almost laughable since there was nothing to be jealous about; on the other hand, it gave her a pleasant chill to think that maybe there could be.

A breeze teased her hair, the filtered sunlight was warm, and she swore when she reached the Student Union and saw that the dining room was closed. Sunday. Short hours, and too bad if anyone missed the posted meals. Now she'd have to wait for dinner.

It was then that she realized how silent it was, as if everyone had left and no one had told her.

Puzzled, she walked on, cutting between the next two buildings to the back where she saw, to her left, a handful of girls halfheartedly doing exercises. To her right, down the slope toward the playing fields, two other girls were walking with heads down, talking, not laughing.

Jennifer knew none of them.

Her stomach complained again, and she slapped at it lightly, turned around, and decided this would be a good time to see what she could learn about the old science building—it was about the only thing she was sure of anymore, and the more she thought about it, the more she refused to believe that it and Grace were not somehow connected.

She tried the library first.

No students were there, and she didn't unearth any books or pamphlets on Thaler's history.

The next step would be to talk to one of the instructors. Most of them were pleasant enough, and she didn't see the harm in asking a few questions, all perfectly innocent from the new girl on campus.

Half an hour later, however, she was growing slightly uneasy.

She had made the rounds of all the buildings and had even walked past the houses where some of the faculty stayed. No one was around. No students, no teachers, not even the slinking Briggs was anywhere to be seen. When she returned to the dorm, the exercise session was over, and the two girls she'd seen heading for the fields were gone. There wasn't even a bird's call to break the silence marked by the hiss of the slow wind over the grass.

Oh lord, she thought, I'm in trouble. Something was going on, something that involved most of the school, and she hadn't been told. She checked quickly in the Student Union foyer, but could find no notice of a meeting, a trip, a service, anything that would explain why, suddenly, the school was so empty.

Her footsteps were too loud on the tiled floor, and she hurried back outside, shading her eyes against the light and gasping when she saw a dark figure moving up the drive.

Lee! She had completely forgotten he was coming that day.

Relief allowed her to relax against a squared post, but tension straightened her when she recognized the figure as the dean.

A smile, then, when he nodded a greeting, changed direction, and moved toward her.

He was wearing a dark shirt and pants, without a suit jacket, and for the first time she saw how fit he was. No doubt about it, she thought. He was as handsome as any man she'd ever seen.

"Good afternoon, Jennifer," he said with a brief smile.

"Good afternoon, Dean Dramon," she said, wondering why she felt as if she ought to curtsy in his presence.

Never taking his eyes from hers, he said, "Not the best of Sundays, is it?"

"It's not too bad," she said, wishing frantically for an excuse to get away."

"Quiet. The student body has escaped into Staines."

"Yes," she whispered. Could it be as simple as that?

Continuing to look at her, he smiled again. "Miss Field, is something the matter?"

"No," she answered hastily. "No, nothing at all."

"Is it Miss Korder?"

She nodded once, not daring to speak.

"A tragedy," the man said, clasping his hands behind him. He looked out over the commons, breaking his hold on Jennifer. "A sad thing when one so young has passed."

He was still two steps below her, on the drive, and she couldn't help looking more closely at the line of his broad shoulders, the thickness of his black hair, snapping her head away when he turned to look at her again.

"I assume you're preparing yourself for next week?"

She gave him a faint shrug. In ten days the session would end with a series of intensive examinations that would decide whether all her work would be credited for the coming semester. She was shocked to realize how quickly the month had gone, and at how she hadn't even given the tests a single thought.

"I understand that Mrs. Gantrel is rather pleased with your work."

Jennifer continued to meet his gaze, and before she could stop herself she said, "Mr. Dramon, what's that lab for, the one in the old science building?"

Dramon stared, his mouth partly open. "Lab?"

Had she somehow found the nerve, she would have run then—back to her room, to pack and leave. She couldn't believe she had been so stupid as to blurt out her question like that. Though if the dean didn't know about it, who would?

She lifted her head, made her spine rigid. "Yes, sir, the lab in the science building. The one out in the woods."

"You saw it?"

She was so relieved she could have hugged him, but not so much that she lost all caution. She nodded. "It was when Lee Fawkes and I found Grace the other day. We'd been walking, and we found her, and . . ." Her hands felt suddenly wet. "I was trying to find out why she'd do such a dumb thing, going out there and all. I ended up at the building, and—"

Dramon abruptly broke into a dazzling grin. "And you were curious, and you looked around, and you found a laboratory."

She nodded. "Yes, that's right!"

He chuckled, briefly rubbed the back of his neck, and stepped up from the drive, took her arm before she could move away, and said, "Miss Field, I guess it was bound to happen. I think, then, you and I had best have a little talk."

Though his grip wasn't hard, she knew she'd never be able to break away if she tried, and she allowed herself to be walked along the covered walks until they reached the administration building—high arched windows, the brick darker than on the other structures, the double front doors at least nine feet high. He opened one and waved her in, followed and closed the door firmly behind them.

There was air conditioning, and it was almost cold as they walked across a white marble floor beneath a huge crystal chandelier. The ceilings were high, the walls covered with oils of the academy's previous administrators, and a fan-shaped staircase lay straight ahead. Beside it was a hallway down which the dean brought her, to a thick oak door beyond which was a massive room with walls lined with books, a floor that was richly carpeted, and furniture that was large, black leather, and dominated by a massive walnut desk.

Dramon sat behind it and gestured her into a chair.

She felt small in such an outsized room and out of place in the midst of such obvious richness. The only other time she'd been in this building was when she had registered, and at that time she was only shown the various offices that flanked the center hall. They were ordinary and certainly gave no indication that a room like this existed.

She was also frightened. There was something about the way the man leaned back in his thronelike chair and regarded her thoughtfully. She squirmed, and he smiled.

"You're not in trouble, Miss Field, if that's what you're concerned about. Though," he added somewhat sternly, "I do wish you had curbed your natural curiosity. You might have injured yourself, or disrupted something very vital."

"Mr. Dramon," she said, "I just wanted—"

"I know, I know," he said, waving her silent. "And as long as you've found out, I suppose the others have as well."

She said nothing. She didn't have to—she knew it was written all over her face.

He tented his long fingers under his chin and thought for a moment. Then, his tone pleasant: "Thaler, Miss Field, is well off, as you may have already gathered. It is not, however, so well off that it can afford to refuse reasonable outside assistance when it is offered. That laboratory—which is Mrs. Gantrel's pet project, as I'm sure you know—is the source of some rather delicate research she has been asked to perform."

She nodded and said nothing, her hands clasped tightly in her lap. Right then she wanted nothing more than to have Lee barge in and demand to know what was going on, or to have Monica waltz through the door with her eyes all wide and innocent and ask the dean if she could borrow Jenny for a while. Anything. A fire, an earthquake, anything to get her out of there.

"You're worried," the man said. "Don't be. We're not talking about millions of dollars of Defense Department dirty tricks here. There are no lasers, no poison gases, nothing like that at all." He smiled, lowered his hands and placed them on the desk. "I can assure you there is no danger to you or your friends, and, more importantly, it had nothing to do with Grace Korder's passing."

She met his gaze, saw the corners of his mouth twitch, and decided an earthquake was too simple. It would be better if the ground just opened up and swallowed her.

"Dean Dramon," she said, "I'm really sorry. But I wasn't snooping. I was just trying to find out about Grace, and—"

He stood and came around the desk, took her by the arm and brought her to her feet. "Miss Field," he said as he led her to the door, "you have no idea what a pleasure it is to have a woman such as yourself at Thaler. I'm afraid many of the others are a little filled with themselves because of their families and positions. You are, if I may say so, a breath of refreshingly clear air."

She didn't know what to say. She felt herself blushing, heard herself stammering, and the next thing she knew she was standing alone in the center hall, shivering from the air conditioning and wondering why she'd been so frightened.

It wasn't until she was outside again that she remembered something the man had said.

"Mrs. Gantrel's pet project, as I'm sure you know . . ."

Someone called her name.

She did know, of course, that Gantrel had something to do with what was out there—but how did the dean know it? How did he know she had connected the woman with the lab?

Footsteps on the drive, and a voice calling to her, demanding her attention.

She turned to stare at the doors, and despite the season she felt a chill that raised goose flesh on her arms.

How did he know?

Then someone grabbed her shoulders and spun her around. She started to break free, then nearly dropped in relief.

It was Lee.

"Jenny," he said, his face flushed from running, his hair matted with perspiration. "Jenny, we've gotta talk."

Her mouth opened, closed, and her eyes blinked rapidly.

"Jenny, are you all right?"

She was able to nod, but only barely. "The dean," was all she could say.

"Yeah," he said. "That's what I gotta talk to you about. Jenny, you were right. Something's going on, and it isn't good."

Chapter Eleven

SHE CONTINUED TO STARE AT HIM, HER confusion growing. "What are you talking about?" she asked.

He looked at her, looked at the doors of the administration building, and shook his head in disgust. "Well, I'm not going to tell you here, that's for sure. C'mon." He took her hand and pulled until she followed, back toward her dorm. "The place is like a graveyard," he muttered. "What do you rich guys do on Sundays, anyway? Fly to Paris or something?"

She started to explain that most students took the opportunity to walk into town, but then stopped, annoyed. "Hey, wait a minute," she protested.

"Sorry," he said gruffly. "I forgot."

She nodded, accepting what she assumed was a poor excuse for an apology.

At the end of the Student Union he hesitated. "I suppose we can't go to your room, right?"

"Are you kidding?"

"Didn't think so. Stupid rule, if you ask me."

Finally, she yanked her hand free. "Look, do you have something to tell me or not?"

He glared, abruptly softened his expression, and with a wave, ducked into the space between buildings where, midway down, he slumped against the wall and let himself slide to the grass. He kept blowing at the hair falling into his eyes. He was wearing a black Windbreaker, faded jeans, and a pair of well-worn tan western boots. His swagger was gone, replaced by angry bewilderment. She stood over him until he looked up, gave her a half-hearted grin, and patted the ground beside him. When she knelt, sitting back on her heels, he immediately looked away again, shaking his head slowly.

"I just talked to the dean," she told him. It was obvious he was having trouble with what he wanted to say, and she decided she might as well give him her news first.

"You did what?"

"I asked him about the lab."

He looked at her slowly. "What lab?"

It took her several seconds to remember that he hadn't been told about the previous night's expedition. Before he could ask the question again she explained what she and her friends had discovered in the woods and, with some reluctance, what she thought she had seen both in the old building and in the infirmary. She thought he would laugh. She wished he would.

Finally he said, "And you told the dean you knew about all this?"

"Sure, why not? All this sneaking around was driving me crazy. So I just asked him."

"Just like that?"

She grinned. "Just like that," and she explained what Dramon had told her about the research grant, and how reasonable it all seemed until she wondered how the man had guessed she knew about Mrs. Gantrel. "The only thing I can think of," she said, "is that she saw me. But if she saw me, recognized me, why didn't she say anything? Why didn't she come after me right away if it's all such a big secret?"

"Oh, great," he said and looked at the sky as the overcast was slowly shading to slate. "I just don't believe this."

"Believe what?" She grabbed his shoulder and forced him to look at her. "Lee, I can't read your mind. If you don't talk to me, how am I supposed to know what you're talking about?"

"Yeah, well . . . I think," he said at last, "there's something going on out here, something bad, Jen. Something very bad."

She closed her eyes, not wanting to hear it. Suddenly she felt very cold and very small and wanted nothing more than to be a little girl again, to be able to crawl into her father's lap where all the terrors of the world were swiftly erased by the comforting sound of his voice, banished and buried by a story and a laugh.

"Jen?"

"I'm okay," she said, not feeling okay at all. "Just a little spooked, that's all."

"Join the club," he said with a forced laugh.

She squirmed around until she faced him.

"So?" "So," he said. "So yesterday I got home, had supper, and was thinking about today. You know."

She grinned and nodded.

"So, anyway, I was going to call you last night, but I forgot when I heard the sirens. You probably can't hear them out here, but there was a fire downtown, see, a small one, no big deal, in the Hilltop, the coffee shop by the theater. You know where it is?"

"Yes. I think they make their hamburgers out of the tar left over from paving the street."

"That's it, all right." But his laugh was short. "Jen, in a small town like Staines, when you get a fire, everybody goes, you know what I mean? If you can't do anything to help, then you hang around and watch." He looked at her sideways with an abrupt sheepish grin. "Hey, it isn't the most exciting thing in the world, I know, but—"

"Lee," she said, "it's all right." She squeezed his hand. "I know, believe me. Staines isn't all that much smaller than the town I come from."

His nod was crisp, but he wouldn't meet her eyes. And in that moment, Lee trying so terribly hard not to tell her what he thought was so important but knowing he had to no matter how much she might be hurt, she felt a rush of affection so strong that it made her catch her breath.

"Go on," she whispered when she could talk without her voice breaking. "What is it, Lee? What about the fire?"

He blinked slowly, once, and she knew that he understood that it would be all right. She wasn't going to hate him just because he brought her bad news.

"Right," he said, his voice tight and harsh. "So, anyway, I got talking to one of the cops I know, and I asked him, I don't know why, about all the trouble out here. About Grace and all, I mean." He took a deep breath and did look at her then. "Jen, he didn't know what I was talking about."

It took her a second to understand, and another to find the words. "What? What do you mean, he didn't know? How could he not know, for heaven's sake?"

"Look, I know it sounds crazy, but he honestly didn't know a thing about what had happened. I thought at first maybe that was all right, nothing to get worked up about. Cops don't always tell each other what's going on. So I went to another guy, one I knew was on the day shift, and when I asked him, he told me the same thing."

"Impossible."

"No, it's not, Jen. If all the cops came out here yesterday that you said, one of those guys would have heard about it."

She didn't know how long she sat there on the damp grass, feeling the wind bringing another storm, listening to the blood race in her ears. But Lee didn't say anything, for which she was grateful. She had to think. She had to go over his story and try to discover where it fell apart, a place she could point to and prove that he was wrong. Maybe he had asked the wrong questions, or gotten confused about the answers. There was a fire, after all, and a lot of excitement and people running around and fire engines and things. It would be easy to mistake what someone had told him for what he thought he heard.

But she didn't believe it.

Her instincts and reason told her not to believe it.

"Jen?"

She waved him silent and covered her eyes, trying to get her thoughts back into one place.

"Jen!" he said quietly, insistently, and pointed when she looked up.

Someone was standing in the opening between the buildings, his back toward them, his arms stiff at his sides. The clouds had continued to thicken, the air touched now with the first hints of fog as the temperature slowly dropped, and the tall figure was dark against the unearthly shimmer of green as the grass stubbornly held on to its bright color.

Neither of them moved, and neither dared speak.

It was Peter Dramon, and he stood motionless for several long minutes before striding straight across the open ground until he paused, then swerved sharply left and disappeared from view.

Jennifer sensed the man had known they were here.

"What's he doing, sneaking around like that?" Lee said.

"I don't know," she answered and dismissed the dean with a chop of her hand. "It doesn't make any difference. I don't care. What's important now is that I was told there was practically a convention of police and ambulances out here yesterday. And that's wrong. It was . . . it was a lie!"

"You mean you didn't see them?"

"No, I didn't." She took his hand again and rubbed its back, held it tightly. "I was . . . those drugs. I was spaced."

"Yeah, I know. So spaced out you thought I was a werewolf or something."

"Right," she said. "I wasn't aware of anything. I could have been in Russia for all the good I was."

"Then who told you about it?"

"Monica," she said instantly. "And Marysue." Her eyes closed, and she felt the first sting of tears. "Oh, no, if you're right, they lied to me, Lee. They lied to me!"

She jumped to her feet and would have run off if Lee hadn't scrambled after her and grabbed her hand. Then he stood, and before she knew what he was doing, put his arms around her and held her close.

"There's an explanation," he said as she laid her cheek against his chest. "There has to be an explanation, or why would your friends lie like that? Maybe it was the drugs, Jen. I mean, maybe you thought you knew what they were saying, but you got it all confused."

She didn't know.

For a moment she didn't think she knew anything at all.

What had started out as a simple quest for under-standing had now become a terrible nightmare, made all the worse because she wasn't asleep. She couldn't wake up and find herself in her room, with everything and everyone back to normal. She couldn't laugh it off, and she couldn't pretend it hadn't happened.

A window opened in the dorm, and a blare of music exploded over the campus, was cut off when someone shouted a protest, and the window was soon closed.

Out on the highway a truck's airhorn sounded, was followed almost at once by a tremendous series of backfires that echoed off the buildings like a round of cannon.

The silence that returned was nearly painful in contrast.

Suddenly Jennifer drew back without leaving the pro-tection of his arms. "Lee," she said, "if nobody came from the hospital to get Grace, where is she?"

The wind gusted around the building, making them duck their heads until it had passed. There was the smell of rain and the knowledge that the storm was just waiting behind the hills, taking its time, knowing that sooner or later it would drive everything to cover.

"I think we ought to call the cops," Lee said when they could talk again.

She nodded instantly, then groaned and slumped against him again. That would be the perfect solution—call the police, tell them all they knew, and stand aside while justice was done.

"What's the matter?" he asked.

"We can't."

"Can't what? Call the cops?" He tried to push her back in order to see her face, but she clung all the more tightly and shook her head instead.

"Think, Lee," she said. "Think."

It was a great idea. The trouble was, what would they tell them? A girl had died and her body was missing, but it seemed that no one in authority at the academy had bothered to notify anyone off-campus. How could they believe that? She would tell them, then, that Briggs the custodian and Miss Hoburn the nurse had seen the body and had brought it to the infirmary. But Miss Hoburn and Jennifer's so-called friends would most likely deny lying about the ambulance, the police, and everything else.

Without a body she couldn't even prove Grace was dead at all. They would just say Grace was a runaway.

She could just imagine what the police would say about that, especially, she thought, when they learned she had been given a sedative for her nerves and had had a reaction, one that blurred reality into nightmare.

"I don't know what to do," she said. "I don't know what to do."

He looked blindly over her head and inhaled slowly. "Grace. If the cops are going to believe us, we have to find out what they did with Grace."

Chapter Twelve

JENNIFER LEFT LEE BY THE DORM'S FIRE DOOR and ran upstairs to get a jacket for protection against the rain that would surely come before they were done. As she yanked it on hastily, she saw again the Thaler yearbook and remembered what had eluded her before. Quickly she flipped over the first few pages to find a photograph of a distinguished-looking elderly man who seemed to have more hair above his eyes than on his scalp. John Innlake, the academy's former dean and, she thought, just the man to ask about the new administration. He lived, if Monica had been right, in Staines.

Her jacket on, she ran back to the hall, hesitated, then knocked on both Marysue's and Barbara's doors. No one answered, nor did Monica respond when she tried hers. There was music, faint and classical, but nothing more, and she shrugged away a fresh stab of hurt at their deception, and she vowed that the answers would come with or without their help.

She was halfway down the stairs when she decided she might need a light. She swung around and ran back to Marysue's door, tried it, and found it open. The flashlight was on the desk, but she couldn't help but take a quick look around, her lips tight, her eyes dark. There was nothing out of the ordinary. It looked, in fact, just like her room, except there were enlarged prints on the wall of what she assumed were views of Virginia's countryside and the Beauford house.

An urge to go through the desk and chest of drawers was sidetracked when she heard someone singing loudly and off-key in the shower. She tucked the flashlight into her waistband and left, making sure the door was closed firmly behind her.

Lee was leaning impatiently against the wall when she burst through the fire exit. She parted her jacket to show him what she'd brought, and they hurried toward the woods without a single word passing between them.

There was no doubt where they had to look first—the old science building.

And if the iron door was locked, they had decided without speaking it aloud that they would break in.

The wind blew steadily now, picking up fallen leaves and debris to fling in their faces. They ran with their heads down, braced against the first drops of rain they knew would come any minute. Even when they found the path Mrs. Gantrel had used and had plunged into the trees, there was little protection against the pre-storm chill, and she didn't object when, forced to slow down by the close underbrush, Lee put an arm around her shoulders. It was warmth of several kinds, and she was grateful.

Eventually the path forked and narrowed, and she pointed to the right. Lee reluctantly dropped his arm and followed without debate, and they moved on, slower now as thorns whipped against their legs and thighs and the branches overhead clacked and snapped.

The wind rose to a keening.

A raindrop struck the back of her neck with the force of a hard-flung pebble.

When they neared the clearing and could see the building dark in the gloom ahead, they stopped.

Instinctively they dropped into half crouches and moved to the clearing's edge, huddling against the bloated trunk of a high-crowned elm.

"Lee, what are we going to do if we find her?"

A spray of rain turned their heads away, and they both shivered when the rain began lashing through the foliage, blurring the building's outlines and soaking them instantly.

Jennifer held his arm and pulled him close. "Lee?"

"We have to get in first," he told her. "After that, I don't know."

They decided not to bother with the entrance—most likely it was locked, and forcing it would only advertise their presence. Instead, they circled the building through the woods until they reached the other side, and when the wind paused Jennifer pointed at a corner window. He nodded, pulled his collar close around his neck, and rubbed his hands briskly together. Then, with a broad wink, he dashed into the open, Jennifer right on his heels. They didn't try to be silent; the rain was making so much noise that it would drown their approach to anyone inside.

The plywood was nailed shut.

Lee cursed, slammed a fist against the wall, and they ran to the back. When he tried to pry loose the comer window there, she stopped him and pointed to the others farther along. That one, she thought, was too dangerous— it looked in on the lab, and she suspected that was where someone would be if the building was occupied.

He balked, then shrugged, and they tried the next one for a loose edge, then a third one, and looked solemnly at each other when the fourth one gave slightly. If they were really going to go through with it, they would have to do it there. And once in, there was no telling what they might find.

He raised an eyebrow.

She nodded once, firmly.

He ran back to the woods and returned with a stout branch. As she stood at the comer and watched for anyone's approach, he broke the branch in half over his thigh and jammed the resulting wedged end into the gap between plywood and frame. He hesitated, biting his lower lip nervously, then slowly pulled until a nail came loose a third of the way up.

He froze as Jennifer joined him, and when she nodded a second time, he worked his makeshift crowbar along the bottom of the covering until he was able to pull it out several inches.

Again they paused, and again they agreed.

After tossing the branch away, he signaled instructions to her until she understood, wiped the rain vainly from his face, and gave her a now-or-never smile.

She leaned closer, whispered, "Be careful," in his ear, then gave him a kiss on his cheek for luck. He seemed startled and didn't move until she poked him, grabbed the plywood's bottom edge, and pulled it out as far as she could. Immediately he slipped under, grabbed the sill, and hauled himself up. His legs kicked, catching her on the arm, but she held on until he was in and keeping the window open himself.

I can't do it, she thought as he gestured impatiently with his head. I can't go in there.

The rain increased, rising in boiling clouds of steam-like mist from the ground and hiding the woods behind a shifting wall of ghostly gray.

No, I can't do it.

Lee hissed at her and widened his eyes in demand.

Before her courage deserted her completely, she grabbed the sill and climbed up, threw herself over, and half fell, half crawled until she dropped silently to the floor. Lee guided the plywood cover shut and knelt beside her, panting, while he tried to wipe away the water dripping from his hair to his face. Her own breathing was difficult, too, but she was having more of a problem with the waves of cold that set her teeth chattering.

The room was no larger than an ordinary study, as far as she could tell. What light there was came from slight cracks in the plywood, and through a pane of beaded glass in the door on the left-hand wall. It was sufficient, however, to show them that whatever furniture and wall coverings it once had were now gone, long gone by the layer of dust that covered the floor.

Slowly, once she was sure their entrance hadn't been noticed, she made her way to the door, her head tilted to one side, listening for signs of others. But she could hear nothing but the rain and the wind, and by the time she had her hand on the cold brass knob she was almost convinced they were alone.

With a silent prayer and a look at Lee, she opened the door cautiously, wincing each time the rusted hinges protested, until she was able to see clearly into the hall.

It was painted a now stained and streaked white to its high ceiling and stretched the width of the building. There were no lights that she could see, nor places where fixtures might have been, and in several places she could see the glint and sway of large spider webs, which here and there were broken by the husks of long dead prey.

She held out a hand to stop Lee from following and poked her head out. The hall ended at a blank wall in back, at the iron door in front. One door, on the opposite wall, led off it.

When at last she shook herself and stepped over the threshold, she could see there was a stairwell between the room they were in and the next.

And, still, there was silence.

Lee moved out beside her, checked the hallway himself, and gave her a look of disgust before moving off confidently, stopping only when he reached the stairs. A pause, and he looked up and shook his head, disgust now changed to puzzlement. Yet he still did not speak when she looked into the stairwell and saw that it curved out of sight to the left.

Then she pointed—the stairs were clean. They were used.

"Now what?" he whispered, and though she could barely hear him, his voice sounded so loud that she readied herself to run back to the room and slam the door behind her. "Up or down?"

"That must lead to the lab," she whispered back, pointing down the hall to the only door on the opposite wall, behind which lights clearly burned. "I know what's in there, sort of. We'd better go up."

He looked doubtful, but gave her a nod and they started up together. There was no banister, but neither did the stairs creak or groan. And once they realized it, they moved quickly, almost running by the time they reached the top and found themselves in a hallway a mirror image of the one below.

The difference was the dark.

The clouds must have massed even more thickly over the hills because there was virtually no light at all, and it was a while before her eyes adjusted as well as they would. She took out the flashlight, aimed it at the floor and turned it on. It was dim, as if the batteries were dying, but it was sufficient for their purposes if they used it wisely.

Then Lee took it from her hand and, before she could stop him, walked boldly down the hall to try the first door on the left. It opened without a sound. He stepped in, and she held her breath until he reappeared, shrugged and stepped down to the next one. It was locked, and when he pressed close to the glass pane and cupped his hands around his eyes, she could tell he couldn't see a thing.

With a nervous glance behind her, she hurried to join him and saw that the other side of the glass had been covered—either with a sheet of black paper or a coating of black paint. When she glanced back at the room he had checked, he said, "Empty. It's clean, though. Someone swept it, but there's nothing in there."

"I don't understand," she said, feeling the first stirring of doubt. "I don't understand."

Taking back the flashlight, she walked over and looked in. Again, the walls and floors were bare but, as Lee had said, free of dust.

Their caution lessened then as they moved past the stairs toward the front rooms. With a look at Lee, she reached for the knob.

And jumped to one side, swallowing a scream, when someone said, "What the hell are you doing here?"

Lee whirled as the fading beam bounced wildly over the walls and ceiling, and finally passed over the flushed face of Daniel Briggs. The custodian squinted but didn't turn away.

"I asked you a question," he said, the words slightly slurred.

Lee cast a silencing look at Jennifer and pulled her under one arm. "Just looking," he said with a faint sneer. "What's the matter, is there a law against it?"

"You ain't supposed to be here," the custodian said and took a step toward them.

"All right, no sweat," Lee said, moving to his right and taking Jennifer with him. "We'll leave, okay? No big deal."

Briggs stared as they sidled past him, stared and followed slowly.

Jennifer wondered where the man had come from. If the iron door had opened they would have heard it, and all the other rooms were locked. Except the laboratory.

"No," Briggs said then.

Lee's arm tightened briefly, then loosened and slipped away, and she knew he was giving her a chance to run when she could.

"What do you mean, no?" the boy said. "I told you we were just looking around, and now we're going. Okay? So we're going. Don't get yourself all—"

Jennifer had no time to scream when Briggs crossed the distance between them in a single stride and grabbed the front of Lee's jacket. Lee struck out furiously, but the custodian ignored the blows on his shoulders and face and lifted him off the ground, shook him and threw him against the wall.

"Lee!" she shouted and ran to him as he slid to the floor, groaning and holding his head. "Lee, are you—"

Briggs snatched the flashlight from Lee's hand and threw it down the hall, reached down and grabbed the boy's arm, and hauled him to his feet. Jennifer, torn between terror and rage, lashed out with a foot against the man's shin and was snared herself by his free hand.

"You're not supposed to be here," he repeated and dragged them down the hall to the door that had to look down into the lab on the first floor. He opened the door while holding Jennifer with his forearm across her neck. "In," he ordered, pushed Lee across the threshold, and glared at Jennifer until she stumbled after, rubbing her neck gingerly.

The door slammed behind them.

And a voice that seemed to come from a great distance said, "Well, well, well, if it isn't the thug and the church mouse."

Chapter Thirteen

A STRONG, STRANGELY FAMILIAR ODOR ALMOST gagged her as she took a deep breath, and her throat burned where Briggs's arm had pressed against it. Wrinkling her nose, she massaged her neck gently and swallowed several times to try to soothe it while she told herself that what she was seeing now was not a dream, not part of her nightmare.

She was standing on a narrow, metal grille catwalk midway up the laboratory's paneled wall, an iron bar railing the only thing between her and an eleven-foot drop to the floor. Lee was slumped on the catwalk beside her, holding his head and moaning softly. An area on the back of his head was matted, blood laying a red background behind the hair, and the area was getting larger, moving toward his neck. She knelt beside him, a comforting hand on his shoulder as she looked beneath the railing to the floor below.

All was as she had seen it before when she had come with Marysue—the cloth-covered tables, the beakers and vials filled with colorless liquids or standing empty over unlighted Bunsen burners, the lights in brackets on the walls, and dozens of shelves neatly arranged with scattered volumes and gear she knew she would recognize if only she had a moment to think.

Yet the equipment was all slightly different, just enough to prevent her from confidently putting names to the items. The idea sent a shudder along her spine she could not stop.

She shifted and saw along the wall opposite her several glass cases six feet high and at least that wide, edged in steel and topped with transparent tanks she thought were empty. She hadn't seen this wall before because the window she had looked through was on it. Each of the cases was connected to the next by a series of hosings, each fronted by a rank of large dials which, she guessed, must regulate the moisture and air purity within.

For the plants.

Dozens of plants that crowded one another for space along the glass walls, reaching to the tops of their enclosures effortlessly—ivy, ferns of all sizes, saplings of nearly every tree she knew, grasses, and scores of flowering shrubs she'd never seen before.

Curiosity moved her to the catwalk's edge, one hand still on Lee's shoulder, the other holding the iron railing for balance.

The last case was unlike the others—twice as wide, twice as deep and, oddly, filled halfway with water, its surface coated with a faint green she assumed was a massive colony of algae or plankton. There were no fish that she could see, no waving stalks of sea plants on the bottom.

Then she recognized the smell that had almost choked her—it was like that of a greenhouse or a florist's, that sweet, almost sickly fragrance that came from the mingling of dozens of different plants.

And at the back the silver oval case.

From her place above the floor it looked chillingly like the nose cone of a rocket that had burrowed up through the floor, except that there was, in its center, what looked like a large porthole the height of a grown man. The capsule's face dripped with condensation, and she couldn't see if anything was inside, but a swift glance showed her that each of the glass cases was, in some way, connected to that menacing chamber.

All this she took in within the space of a few seconds, before she looked down to the room's center.

To Nurse Hoburn in her white uniform, wearing plastic gloves and holding a vial.

"I hope," the woman said, "you're not hurt. Mr. Briggs can sometimes lose his temper over the silliest things." She craned her neck. "You really aren't hurt, are you?"

Lee slumped to his side, and Jennifer saw a trickle of blood snake across his neck.

She was more angry now than afraid, and she rose to her feet and gripped the railing hard. "Who are you?" she demanded. "What are you doing here?"

Hoburn laughed merrily and placed the vial carefully on a table beside her. "I think, my dear, that questions belongs to me." She pointed, and her expression grew abruptly harsh. "If you don't want to see Briggs again, you'll tell me now how you come to be here."

Jennifer looked around as if hunting for something to throw, then lunged for the doorknob, grabbed it and yanked. It was locked. She yanked again and kicked it.

"Unless you can fly," Hoburn said, "you're not going anywhere, my dear."

"You've got to let us go!" Jennifer said, nearly yelling. "Lee is hurt. He needs help!"

"He will live," the woman said. "For the time being."

And it was less the words the nurse spoke than the flat way she said it that drained the anger from Jennifer's system and warned her that this woman, for whatever reasons, would not think twice about having -her killed. If she didn't kill her herself.

Then a door opened below, and Jennifer looked through the grille and saw Mrs. Gantrel stalk in.

"That's taken care of," the teacher said with a dusting of her hands. "Nothing like a good fire to get rid of garbage, I always say. All we have to do now is think of something to tell her guardians when they—" She stopped and frowned. "Amanda, what's the matter?"

Hoburn looked up. Mrs. Gantrel followed her gaze and stepped quickly into the room.

"I see," she said. "What does she know?"

Trembling, Jennifer shook her head.

Hoburn stripped off the gloves. "Now? Everything."

Grace, Jennifer thought. Oh, Grace, I'm sorry. I'm so sorry we didn't talk.

"This is all your fault," Gantrel said angrily, pulling off her trench coat and throwing it on a stool.

"Don't blame me," the nurse protested hotly. "I do what you tell me, nothing more."

The two women began to confer in whispers, and Jennifer took the moment to kneel by Lee again. He was unconscious, breathing steadily, but the flow of blood from beneath his hair had not stopped. Rotating slowly on her heels, she stared along the catwalk, knowing there had to be some way down, or out.

She saw it then, down by the silver capsule—a series of metal rungs set into the wall and leading down. It was, however, too far away to do her any good; and even if a miracle left her in the room alone, she couldn't carry Lee down. For all she knew, he had suffered a concussion and shouldn't be moved.

Despair engulfed her, and she sank down to the grille, drew her knees up, and wrapped her arms around them. She was going to die, she just knew it. Lee was going to die. Dean Dramon knew about the laboratory, but couldn't know that the people he had trusted were . . . what? Agents? Spies? What?

Or had she stumbled into one of those horrible stories she'd seen both on television and in the movies—a secret government agency conducting secret experiments, and whether you were a countryman or not, discovery meant death. In that case, how innocent was Dramon?

She looked down when the women parted, Gantrel toward the door and Hoburn toward a metal cabinet next to the boarded window Jennifer had looked through.

A sob escaped her. She couldn't even depend on her friends anymore because they had lied to her; they were in league with these people; they were part of them.

Whoever they were.

The door slammed shut. Gantrel had left.

A bubbling sound came from Lee's throat; she leaned closer and saw his eyelids flutter weakly. Then, before she could back away, he uttered a low moan and opened his eyes, saw her and tried to speak. A finger against his lips quieted him, and she nodded toward the floor. The way he squinted dismayed her, but he rolled to a sitting position and held the back of his head while he looked around, his lips pursed in a silent whistle. Then he took his hand away and stared at a palm smeared with his still-oozing blood.

"Did I get him?" he asked in a low voice.

She shook her head, wanting to cry, wanting to laugh now that he was back with her.

"Didn't think so."

Slowly, painfully, he grabbed onto the railing and pulled himself to his feet. He leaned over, leaned back, and slouched against the wall. His eyes closed again, and

Jennifer thought he was half unconscious again, until he reached out for her hand.

"Trouble, right?"

She told him about Gantrel.

"No."

Hoburn turned away from the cabinet, and Jennifer gasped when she saw the gun in the woman's hand.

"You will come down now," the nurse ordered, waving her gun hand toward the rungs. "If you are careful, nothing will happen."

"What if we're not?" Lee said loudly.

Hoburn cocked the hammer and simply smiled.

Lee looked in the direction of the door, and Jennifer shook her head sadly, put a supporting arm around his waist, and moved along the catwalk toward the back. Their heels were loud on the metal, clanging, faintly echoing, and she could feel Hoburn's gaze following their every move. At the rungs, which came through a gap in the grille, she hesitated, then began climbing down, gripping each one tightly because it was slick with moisture. At her back she could feel the looming presence of the capsule, and an odd tingling as if it gave off a feeble aura of electricity. Lee came after her much more slowly, and she was already on the floor when he was only halfway down.

"Hurry!" the nurse ordered when Lee paused to look around.

"He's hurt," Jennifer snapped. "Give him a chance."

Hoburn only smiled again, not moving save for the pointing of the gun. "He will be hurt worse if he doesn't hurry up."

Lee muttered something, reached the floor and stood swaying slightly. "He must've hit me with a tire iron," he whispered, and she could tell by the way he closed his eyes tightly, opened them and blinked, that his vision wasn't clear.

"Over here now," Hoburn told them, pointing beside her with the gun.

Carefully they threaded their way around the tables, Jennifer trying desperately to make some sense of what she was seeing. But even now she could make out only a few things—stoppered vials of acids, one of sodium covered in oil, one of dingy yellow sulphur she recognized even without the oddly lettered label.

"We didn't do anything, you know," Lee said, trying to regain some of his usual swagger. "We were just looking around."

Hoburn said nothing.

Jennifer studied the plant cases as she passed them, wondering what Mrs. Gantrel could be doing with them. There was something odd about the green of the leaves, about the thickness of the stalks and stems, but before she could think about it the nurse snapped her name and ordered her against a wall, into a gap between the cabinet and a table that pushed out into the room.

"You wait," she said, settling herself on a high stool.

"For what?" Lee demanded. "I told you we weren't doing anything."

"Please," Jennifer said, her original fear almost conquered by the need to know what this was all about. "What about Grace? What did you do with her?"

Hoburn's eyes narrowed.

"I talked to the dean today," she went on. "He told me about the lab here. It's not a secret anymore so why—"

Hoburn got to her feet, the gun aimed at the middle of Jennifer's chest. "He told you?"

"Sure he did," Lee said. "What's the big deal? You're not making poison gas or anything, right?"

"Poison gas?" Hoburn gaped at him, then began to laugh, a low running laugh that sounded so much like an animal's growling that Jennifer took Lee's arm. "Gas?" The laughter climbed, this time close to a howling, and Jennifer felt a deep chill settle in her blood.

Suddenly the hall door burst open and Gantrel came in, struggling with the weight of Briggs in her arms. The man was gasping for air, his face pale, his clothes in disarray. "Here!" she ordered Hoburn. "Here, help me!"

The nurse glared at Lee, waved the gun at Jennifer, and rushed over to grab Briggs's other arm. Together the two women walked the slumping man toward the capsule in back, muttering until Gantrel shook her head angrily.

"Chasing them," she said. "Too much exertion."

Hoburn looked over her shoulder. "But we can't."

Gantrel left the nurse to work at a hatch wheel on the capsule's side. "No choice. He dies, otherwise."

Jennifer plucked at Lee's side when she realized that whatever the emergency was, it had temporarily removed the threat of Hoburn's gun. Slowly, then, she sidled out of the gap, looked at Lee and almost groaned—he was conscious, but only barely, staring around him as if he were in a daze. They couldn't run, then. If she tried, she might escape, but Lee never would. There would have to be something else, something that would—

Desperately she scanned the closest table. The acids were useless because the women were too far away. To throw one bottle and miss would mean Hoburn would have time to bring her gun to bear. Then she saw it and grabbed it and held it behind her.

The hatch was open, and Gantrel was wrestling the groaning custodian inside. Hoburn, meanwhile, had tucked her gun away and was working over a bank of toggles just below the round window.

"What are they doing?" Lee whispered and fell lightly against her. He righted himself, but only with great effort.

"I don't know," she said. "I don't—"

Then a face appeared in the capsule window, and Jennifer screamed.

Chapter Fourteen

HER FIRST THOUGHT WAS IT ISN'T HUMAN.

The face and figure pressed against the port was fogged by condensation on the glass, but she could see enough to recognize some of the custodian's features until, suddenly, they all changed.

She gripped Lee's arm tightly, just barely keeping herself from screaming again.

In the space of only a few seconds, the man's eyes had become slanted and tinged a faint green, his hair had grown thicker and longer, and his skin peeled off in bloodless, plasticlike strips to reveal a darker layer beneath, which, when the face pulled back, she thought looked almost like fur. An animal's fur.

"Oh, no, Lee," she said, staggering back with him until the edge of a table stopped them. "Oh, no, what is it?"

Lee grunted, a hand rubbing fiercely at his eyes.

And when the creature—she could in her horror no longer think of it as anything else—pulled and tore at its coveralls and shirt, the body it revealed had slimmed, its shoulders had broadened and slightly hunched, and it looked like nothing so much as a forest animal rearing on its hind legs.

Then its hands swept over the glass, momentarily wiping away the moisture, and she could see it clearly for the first time.

It was a wolf.

A wolf with a face that looked distinctly intelligent.

Then the glass fogged over again, and she watched openmouthed as the shadow-figure reared back its head and gulped at the air inside, holding its chest and filling its lungs. It stepped away for a moment and was gone, returned and pressed its dark palms to the glass.

The eyes looked across the room, directly at her.

Green eyes narrowed in undisguised hate. Undisguised hunger.

Jennifer could no longer contain herself. "What *is* it?" she screamed, and Hoburn whirled from the control board, started for her and collapsed against a table. A beaker toppled and spilled pale blue liquid over the stained cloth; test tubes in a rack rattled against one another and threatened to spill as well.

"I can't," the nurse gasped, pulling at her clothes. "Help me. Help me, I need to—"

"Do it yourself," Gantrel snarled and grabbed the gun from the woman's pocket.

"No!" Jennifer yelled and shoved Lee to the floor just as Gantrel fired. The bullet smashed into the shelves behind her, shattering an empty bottle. Another round gouged a trough out of the table just over her head, and Jennifer looked around wildly for a way to escape, looked at her hand and saw the bottle she'd picked up only a few moments before.

It contained small pieces of sodium covered in oil, and she knew there was only one thing she could do with it—if she weren't killed in the process.

But she had no choice. Lee was still dazed and couldn't run on his own, and it was clear they were going to die unless she tried something, and tried it now.

Gantrel fired a third time, smashing glass and showering the floor with sulphur.

A fourth round ripped through the floor by Jennifer's foot, and she knew that there was no time left.

She stood, and in one swift motion drew back her arm and heaved the heavy bottle toward the water case just as the woman fired a fifth time. What felt like a torch pressed against her temple made Jennifer cry out and fall and, at the same time, she heard the bottle smash through the case.

Instantly, there was a blinding flare of fire and a woman's scream as the sodium reacted with the water. Like a hundred flares the light filled the room, and flames leaped to the walls, to the other chemicals, to the tables.

Only a few seconds later virtually every bit of flammable material near the case had ignited, and the roaring filled her ears, the stench had her gagging, and she knew that she had to get Lee out before either gas or fire killed them both.

She took his arms and pulled him to his feet, shouting his name all the while, trying to get through to him, yanking him and stumbling with him toward the door as the fire spread, heat scorching her cheeks and punctuating the roar of the flames with the snap of breaking glass.

Smoke curled and rose toward the high ceiling, then whirled into a tornado as one of the plywood window coverings split apart and the air rushed in from the outside, feeding the fire, driving the smoke into a frenzy, blinding Jennifer as she staggered on, weeping now from the pain in her head and the frustration she felt because Lee could barely walk.

She screamed for help, though she knew no one could hear her, kicked aside a torched stool and could not feel the sparks that landed on her face and hands.

A glimpse of the door before the smoke closed around it, and she made one last lunge with Lee dragging behind her, fell against the wall and scrabbled her hand over the wood until she found the doorknob. She turned it and flung the door open, shoved Lee through, and looked behind her to see if Gantrel had followed.

The far wall was solid flame, and a circle of fire licked and crackled around the silver capsule. She could see a shadow inside beating hysterically against the glass, and could see the open hatch where Amanda Hoburn had started to go in just as the fire broke out. There was no sign of the nurse, but she felt a rumbling beneath her feet and knew it wouldn't be long before there was a powerful explosion.

Then, as the smoke swirled and parted, she saw Gantrel in the middle of the room.

She was surrounded by flame and sinking slowly to her knees; but before the smoke closed again, Jennifer saw the woman's face and one of her hands—wolflike, and covered with dark gray fur.

Then a lash of fire jumped over her head, and she ran into the hall where Lee was slouched against the far wall. She took his hand and pulled him to the iron door, pressed down on the bar and prayed it would open.

It did. And just as she staggered gasping into the rain, the lab exploded and she was flung off her feet, into the darkness.

Wolves pursued her.

Packs of them on four legs, hundreds of them on two legs, wolves that looked as they should, and wolves that looked too much like people, and people she knew.

She ran, knowing she couldn't escape them, but before they overwhelmed her the darkness returned, safe and warm and soon filled with the murmur of friendly voices.

Her eyelids jumped when someone touched her hand, then opened when a cool damp cloth was laid on her brow.

It took a while before she realized she was in a hospital, in a room of soft green with the sun filtering warmly through the open blinds of a window to the right of her bed. There was a bandage around her head, and when she turned to see who had awakened her, Lee pulled his hand back and stuffed it in the pocket of his robe.

"Hey," he said. "Welcome back."

He was in a wheelchair, his face pink from the heat of the fire, and like hers his bandage was wrapped snugly around his brow.

She smiled, then sat up suddenly, remembering all that had happened and feeling a scream working in her throat. Lee leaned over and placed a hand on her arm, still smiling though his eyes shaded with concern.

"It's okay," he said. "It's over. We've both been out overnight. It's Monday, Jen. We're okay."

She looked around the room—into the corner, at the open door to the hallway, at the window. "Safe," she whispered and fell back on her pillow. "Are you all right?"

He shrugged. "Concussion, they said. I keep seeing double, it's a pain." He gazed at her face. "Sometimes."

Annoyed at the blush she felt moving to her cheeks, she looked out the window again, at the hills that seemed to grow right out of the walls.

"You saved my life," he said, clearing his throat. "I, uh, thanks."

She didn't know what to say.

"They said your parents are on the way."

"Oh, good." Then she put a hand to her cheek. "Oh, Lee, what am I going to tell them? What about the police? What—"

He laughed quietly and shook his head. "Don't worry about it, huh? The cops were already here. I told them we were goofing around down there when the place went up."

"Didn't they ask why?"

He looked away, suddenly uncomfortable. "Yeah."

"So what did you tell them?"

He shrugged. "That we were just goofing around, that's all."

"Oh," she said, knowing what the police would think. "Oh." And she surprised herself by not caring what they thought, what anyone thought. It was a good feeling, and a startling one, but she had no time to say anything.

"Hey, look," he said, pushing his chair away from the bed. "I gotta get back. I'm not supposed to be out but I wanted to be sure you were all right. They'll tie me down if they catch me."

"Lee?" she said then, when he reached the door. "What about the lab?"

He looked over his shoulder. "I heard that Dramon told them about some funded experiments that went wrong. Not our fault. Mrs. Gantrel and the others, they died in the explosion."

"But what about what we saw?"

He frowned. "Saw? Saw what?"

"Briggs in that . . . that thing! And—" She stopped and let her eyes close. Lee hadn't seen anything. His vision hadn't cleared in time; she was the only one who knew Mrs. Gantrel and the others hadn't been human.

"Later," Lee said and was gone.

During the next few minutes nurses and interns fussed over her, not giving her time to think, asking about and checking her reactions to light, to sound, and finally pronouncing her well enough to leave as soon as her parents arrived that evening. No one said anything about the fire. No one asked her if she knew what had caused it.

And after some seemingly innocent question, she learned something else—that Grace Korder had never had epilepsy. Hoburn had lied to her, which meant that whatever killed the girl had come from the destroyed lab.

Jennifer remembered Grace was an orphan. With no family to confront, it would be easy to concoct a story to explain her absence to anyone who might ask.

Especially since Hoburn had given her the sedatives deliberately to keep her out of the way when the police were supposed to have come, and hadn't.

It's over, she thought then, Whoever they were, whatever they were, it's all over. The wolf creatures would live now only in her dreams.

There was a light tapping on the jamb, and when she looked over, the smile turned to a grin. The doorway was crowded with faces, nodding to her until she waved them all in—friends from school with well wishes, smiling and making cracks about her and Lee, and carrying so many flowers that there was no place else to put them all.

And laughter.

Most of all there were great peals and gales of laughter that drove away her demons and made her see the sunshine.

She was disappointed when the head nurse finally bustled in and ordered them all out before Jennifer had a relapse, and she felt suddenly very alone as the light in the window began to fade.

She wished Lee would come back.

She wished her parents would hurry up.

And she stiffened when she saw a dark figure in the doorway, waiting hesitantly until, at last, she said, "Come on in."

Marysue Beauford carried a single rose in her left hand, and she placed it by Jennifer's side. Her eyes were red and swollen, and her lower lip trembled. "I thought you were dead," she said, swallowing to keep her voice from cracking. "I thought . . . when I heard about it, I thought you were dead."

Jennifer felt her own eyes filling, and before she knew it they were embracing, crying, then pulling apart in giggling embarrassment.

"I swear, child," the southerner said, "don't you ever pull a stunt like that again, you hear? I like to threw myself out a window in pure despair."

Jennifer wrinkled her nose at her. "No, you wouldn't. It would ruin your nails."

Marysue examined her hands. "Yes, I suppose you're right. I would have punched a pillow, though. Very, very hard."

She laughed, wincing at the pull of the bandages over her scratches and bums, but not caring, not caring at all though it was a while before she could convince herself not to say anything about what she had seen. Lee had been there and had seen nothing; Marysue had been there, and had seen only the lab. To tell her about Gantrel now would be useless. She would only think Jennifer was still feeling the effects of her ordeal.

But there was a question she had to ask, if only to reassure herself that it was really over.

"Marysue, why did you lie about the police and ambulances the day Grace died?"

Marysue looked at her with a puzzled frown. "What are you talking about, girl?"

"You told me the school was crawling with them."

"Well, sure I did. But I never actually saw them."

Jennifer lifted a hand, and dropped it again. "You didn't?"

"No. Monica had told me about them. And then she talked about them in your room later that night, too."

Monica.

But why? she wondered.

And she answered herself: because she's one of them.

She shook her head. Impossible. That couldn't be. But then, she hadn't known about the others either. To her, to the world, they looked perfectly normal.

Monica?

"Marysue, there's something—"

Someone came into the room and stood at the foot of her bed. A flower was tossed into her lap, and a box of candy followed.

"Hey, Field," Monica Holt said. "How are you?"

And as the light faded in the room, Jennifer could have sworn she saw the girl's eyes turn faintly green.

www.ingramcontent.com/pod-product-compliance
Lightning Source LLC
Chambersburg PA
CBHW071958170626
46813CB00005B/1919